MAID O

JP Wagner

This is a work of fiction. Similarities to real people, places, or events are entirely coincidental.

MAID OF THE WESTERMOOR

First edition. July 31, 2022.

Copyright © 2022 J P Wagner.

ISBN: 978-1990862007

Written by J P Wagner.

For Jimmy,

who is just as much a fighter as his grandfather.

Chapter One
THE TENT ON THE BATTLEFIELD

Yesterday it had been a battlefield full of noise and shouting. Today it was a grim and cheerless place. Feasting ravens fluttered and hopped here and there, scavenging beasts glided to and fro, and most of the noise was the moaning of those wounded who were unable to move, and who had neither brother nor friend to help them from the field.

A few tents had been erected for those of rank, and in some of them, men of rank suffered nearly as much as those who lay on the open field.

In one such tent, a young man lay, drowsing from the medicine he had been given for his pain. He was a slender fellow, with neatly trimmed red-brown hair and beard, and a broad face which, though usually friendly, now twisted with pain. His name was Krinneth, son of Darun.

The pain of his wound forced wakefulness on him, despite the sleeping-draught he had been given, and he tried to remember how he had come there. He recalled standing in the hall of his lord, Dhahal son of Dalvin, bending over the sketch-map roughly drawn in charcoal on a trestle-table.

Spring flooding had overfilled a small stream, causing it to cut a new channel, putting a small parcel of Dhahal's land on the far side of the stream. Lord Kevan, who claimed all the land up to the stream, thus laid claim to that patch of ground, whereas Dhahal felt that ownership of land ought not to depend on the whims and chances of the flow of water.

Dhahal was a short and stocky man, a little paunchy, bald from forehead to crown, but with a wide bushy beard to make up for it. He did not look like much, but armed and in armour, he was no mean foe.

"Kevan has driven our cowherds from their pasture twice in the past three days. Tomorrow they go out again, and if Kevan's men are there, why we will be as well."

Had the drug finally taken him down into deep sleep? Suddenly, he was moved from that time to a little later in the evening, when Dhahal had called him aside to talk privately.

"Krinneth, son of Darun, I think it is time we talked. You have served me faithfully for some years now, have you not? As a free knight, you have put your lance at my service and have proven yourself both capable and loyal."

"I am happy to have pleased you, my Lord." What else was there to say to all this?

"Look you, in company you call me 'my Lord.' When we are by ourselves, call me Dhahal. I have a suggestion to make to you."

He paused, almost as though waiting for Krinneth to speak. While Krinneth was trying to decide what sort of response was appropriate, Dhahal went on.

"You have become friendly with my daughter, Gwathlinn, have you not? Yes, I thought so. And I have thought much about this. Suppose I were to offer you the castle of Garkeep? Would you be willing to take it?"

"Garkeep?" Krinneth knew the castle. It was hardly worthy of the term, being little more than a wooden palisade with a stone tower in the center. But even so...

"Yes, Garkeep. It is small, but it is a holding of its own. If you are willing, I could give you Garkeep with my daughter. It is not the most important of my castles, but it is still one which I would like to have in trustworthy hands. What say you?"

"My lord, Dhahal, I know not what to say. You do me much honour."

"Bah! No more than you are entitled to, boy. Look, you think on this, and tell me your answer after tomorrow."

Had he slept again? Suddenly he was among the willows, riding behind Dhahal, his lance in his hand, not upright, but held down and slanting forward so as not to catch in the low branches. They came out of the willows into that little patch of ground, no more than fifty yards across. And Kevan's men were waiting out beyond, men in armour, bright surcoats gleaming with their insignia. Dhahal rode out a little ahead of his men to talk.

What had happened then? Try as he would, he could remember nothing until he had awakened here, in this tent, and had been given something by an old man. He had been wounded, of course, but he bore no memory of himself in the fight.

He slept again.

"My lady, he ought not to be living now. If he lives out the night, it will be a wonder, and if he lives two days, it will be a greater wonder. And if the greatest wonder of all should occur and he survives, he will never be hale again."

"Well, blast you and all your medicines, then! If you can do nothing for him, I will find someone who can!"

The male voice he thought to be that of Dhahal's healer. The female voice was surely Gwathlinn daughter of Dhahal. His eyes would not open, but he could see her in his mind, near as tall as himself, fair of face, with her determined chin set forward. He wondered what clothing she was wearing; she prided herself somewhat in always wearing what was suitable for the occasion.

He wanted to say something, to ask them how they could decide his fate for him as though he were no more than a chunk of meat, but before he could find the words, he had drifted off again into a hazy dream.

He thought once he came to wakefulness, or near wakefulness, and heard Dhahal himself speaking with the same healer.

"No healing for him, then?"

"Probably not. The most we can do is give him a drug to deaden the pain, and even that may not suffice toward the end."

"My daughter is determined that he shall recover."

The shrug of the healer's shoulders was practically palpable to Krinneth in his hazy near-sleep. "Strange things and stranger have happened. If he heals, he will not likely be the man he was. What will you do then, when he can no longer fight for you?"

There was anger in Dhahal's voice. "And am I some near bandit of the hills who keeps his folk only so long as they are of use to him? He has born arms for me, he has scars won in my service, and he has a place at my table for so long as he wishes, be he hale and strong or born about in a litter!"

It was quiet for a time, then Dhahal spoke again. "My daughter is determined to find healing for him. She is seeking for anyone who will promise to make him well."

"If there is money promised, many will make promises, if only to get a little of it. And indeed there are tales of healing powers available, even some reputable witnesses to the operation of such powers. The difficulty is to know when the boasted powers are real and when they are not."

Krinneth slept again and wakened again to swallow another draught of the pain-killing medicine. This time he opened his eyes as well, and in the light of fluttering torches, he saw and heard the low-voiced argument between Gwathlinn and the healer.

"My lady, this is wrong!"

"Wrong? Wrong? Let me tell you what wrong is! Wrong is to let Krinneth suffer, and probably dwindle into a cripple capable of nothing more than sitting by the fire and remembering the days of his health!"

"My lady, on the word of one person, you will take him on this journey, increasing his suffering, with no sure hope of healing at the end of it?"

"Up till the present, no one has given him any hope for healing. I have even heard one person bold enough to say that it would be far better to kill him with a quick dagger-thrust than let him be as he is!

"But my maid tells me that the folk of the hills for years have gone to the Maid of the Westermoor for healing, and there is little left to lose by trying."

"But to trust a being out of Faerie—-"

"I would trust a hunchbacked goblin if there were some hope of having Krinneth made well again! My mind is made up, and I am taking him. You can decide for yourself whether or not you will accompany us."

Krinneth, as he was slipping back into sleep, felt humbly grateful for the love that made her so determined to heal him. He wondered a little at the desperation in her voice, but decided that it must be due to the serious nature of his wounds.

Chapter Two
THE MAID OF THE WESTERMOOR

The litter swung and swayed as the horses moved, and the movement, each footfall of each horse, brought pain to Krinneth. The pain penetrated even through the fog of the draught he had been given, so he slept fitfully, if at all. When they stopped to camp, he would rest, and then he could even feel free enough of pain to consider it fortunate they were moving him in a litter instead of a wagon. The litter swung and moved with the motion of the horses, and it did jar with their footfalls, but those were minor jars compared with the kind of bouncing, slamming ride he would have had in a wagon.

In the evening, Gwathlinn would come and sit with him. She did not try to converse with him, for which he was grateful. When the pain did not make it difficult to think, the pain-medicine made his brain too foggy. He would wake sometimes to see her staring at the wall of the tent, as off into some far distance. The expression on her face said she did not like what she saw there.

She was the youngest of three daughters, and the other daughters of Dhahal were both married and married well. The difficulty for Gwathlinn had been that there were too few young lads in the locality of suitable age and station. Marriages were more often made for political or dynastic reasons than for romantic reasons, but even so, Dhahal was not a man to drive his daughter to an alliance which was totally repugnant to her.

But time had gone by, and there had been no offers for her hand, at least none which her father could countenance. Gwathlinn had been pleased when Krinneth began to pay attention to her, and it seemed his status as a mere knight, though not the highest in the land, was not a trial to her. When this thought came to his mind, he wondered just how much Gwathlinn had had to do with Dhahal's offer of Garkeep.

Even as that thought came to him, he knew Dhahal was not a man to assign any person to a command if he thought they had not earned it, and no amount of badgering from his daughter would be likely to change that.

And yet, when Krinneth came out of his sleep to see her sitting at his side, he wished he could gather his wits sufficiently to ask her what was going on in her thoughts.

HE HAD NO IDEA HOW many days they had been travelling, but he knew from what snippets of conversation he could capture, that they were on the borders of Faerie. The day was bright and fair, so they had pulled back the curtains of his litter that he might enjoy the sun.

The track wound round hillsides and through willow copses, and there was scarce room for the litter to go round some of the sharper corners. The sun was going down when a voice called to them.

"Where do you go, and what do you seek?"

Krinneth himself was in his half-waking state, so he heard the voice, too. He also heard Gwathlinn answer as the party came to a stop.

"We go to seek the Maid of the Westermoor, and we bring a man sore wounded, who needs healing."

Krinneth looked around, seeking the source of the voice, and finally saw an owlet on a willow-branch. The owlet opened its beak, and a voice came from the small owl.

"Go ye toward the setting sun and seek the water's edge. At dawn, let he who seeks the healing go forth, and toss a handful of goldenrod into the water, and wait for what comes."

The owlet lifted from the branch and flew slowly away, leaving the party talking to each other in amazed whispers.

"Enough!" Gwathlinn's voice cut through the babble. "We know we are on the right road. Now let us go forward. You all knew the purpose of this trip; did you expect you would not witness strange things?"

They came to the edge of the mere shortly afterwards and made camp. That evening Gwathlinn came in to see Krinneth, and this time she stayed to speak. "We were greeted this afternoon," she said, "By an owlet, which demanded to know our destination and our business."

"Yes, I heard," he said, and found that even the exertion of speaking caused him pain.

"You heard what he said? Tomorrow morning, you are to go to the edge of the mere and cast in a handful of goldenrod."

"Yes." He clenched his teeth against the pain.

"Yes." She nodded. "I fear you are to suffer more pain, for tomorrow morning we cannot give you the medicine which holds the pain away, for you must be sufficiently awake to carry out the instructions of the Witch."

"I will try to bear it." The pain was only a little easier to bear for being expected.

"Good." She laid a gentle hand on his forehead. "Oh my dear one, I certainly hope that this has not been all for nothing. Hush, hush, I can see it hurts you to talk. Rest, and we shall see what the morning brings."

Krinneth was awake early in the morning, and as Gwathlinn had feared, he was in great pain. Two of the men-at-arms had made a stretcher from cloaks laid over two spear-shafts, and bore him down to the water's edge. In his hand, he clutched a handful of goldenrod and waited.

Finally, the sun's disk was free of the horizon. Krinneth raised his hand to toss the goldenrod out into the mere, and the pain of it was such that he nearly fainted. The bunched and crumpled stems of goldenrod lay floating on the water, and nothing else happened.

Krinneth drew in a careful breath. So this effort was all for nothing, then? He had endured the agony of the journey and the pain of this morning, all to no end?

There was a flash of something deep in the mere, perhaps a fish. Even as he watched, it rose through the water, growing in size. He could not make out what it was yet, then with a last surge, it broke the surface, and he stared in amazement.

Before him on the bank was something strange, something having the body of a black mare and the chest, shoulders and head of a young woman. Water dripped and splashed from her horse-body, ran down out of her long black hair. She turned eyes on him.

"Why come you here?"

"I come for healing." The pain of speaking even those few words was excruciating, and he had to suppress a gasp.

"There is a price for such healing. Will you pay it?"

"Now how can anyone answer that without knowing what the price will be?" Gwathlinn was standing beside him, and he was glad for it, for he was not sure he could have spoken the words she spoke, though he knew the question must be asked.

The woman-horse turned her face to Gwathlinn, and Krinneth continued to regard her. The woman-horse's face was not strikingly beautiful, nor was it particularly ugly. Her nose was large and beakish, protruding from between the eyes, and was matched by prominent cheekbones as well. Her hair was long and black, hanging down to what would have been waist-length on a normal woman. The woman-horse's expression seemed to say that this was a being secure in her own self, not needing to seek approval from anyone.

"You do his speaking for him?"

"If you are not blind, you can see that it pains him to speak. I will talk for him, and if I am not sure how I should answer, I will then ask him. But for prices and payments, I will speak."

The woman-horse stood quietly for a moment, looking into Gwathlinn's face. She nodded briefly, then, and said, "So be it. The price that I ask is nine years' service."

"Nine years? Impossible!"

"Then so is the healing. I do not come here to bargain. The price that I set is the price I will be paid."

"Nine years' service, for an unproven healing?"

"Nine years' service, and if the healing does not succeed, nothing."

Gwathlinn looked from the woman-horse to Krinneth. "Now that is an answer I cannot give, not without speaking to him."

The woman-horse smiled. "I thought as much. Speak to him, then, and I will wait here for your answer."

Gwathlinn turned to Krinneth. "I know you are sworn to my father, but I think he will give you leave for nine years. After all, you can hardly serve him without your health, can you? But this must be your decision."

"Tell her," said Krinneth, "Tell her I agree." And in his mind, he was wondering whether he did indeed think that Dhahal would give him leave, or whether it was just a desire to be free of this pain. The pain surged over him for a moment then, and he heard, faint and far-off, Gwathlinn passing on his answer.

Chapter Three
THE HEALING

The pain subsided sufficiently for Krinneth to pay a little more attention to what was going on. He was glancing at the woman-horse when she changed. The horse-body twitched, the way a horse will do in trying to shake off flies, then continued to ripple and shift. A moment later the horse-body was gone, and what stood before him was a maid, barefoot, with long black hair, clad in a white shift that hung to her ankles.

Her eyes fell on Krinneth where he lay watching her, and she smiled at him as though the two of them shared some sort of secret.

The maid began giving orders and Gwathlinn's party were set to work at building a small hut made of woven reed mats on a frame of poles. The hut was not tall, and a man of average height would have to stoop to enter it. But the makeshift hut was large enough to hold Krinneth's stretcher and another person besides. She said that the doorway must face to the East, so that the first rays of the rising sun would shine into the hut.

The Maid stood watching with impassive features as this was done, saying nothing while they worked. When they had completed the hut, they hung a blanket up in the doorway, then pinned it to one side while they carried Krinneth in.

They laid him down and went out, and Krinneth was not at all surprised to see fear showing on their faces. He was afraid himself, but the pain did not allow him time to be more than half aware of his fear.

After they had left, the Maid came into the doorway, then turned and spoke to Gwathlinn's party.

"By tomorrow morning, he will be healed. From now until he comes forth from the hut, do not come closer than a hundred paces, for your very lives' sakes."

Without waiting for an answer, she let the blanket fall across the doorway, then turned to Krinneth.

"My name is Lithlannon. Yours I know is Krinneth. No, you need not answer. I know it pains you, and you shall have pain enough later on.

"No, I do not hide from you the fact that this healing will hurt. In fact, I suspect that were you to truly know how much it will hurt, you would reject it now."

She smiled at him, a smile which brightened her whole face.

"I begin by frightening you, of course. It is intended. Such healing as you require is not undertaken lightly, and on your part there must be at least determination, if not the ability, to withstand pain.

"No, do not speak. I get answer enough from your face and your body. No, I do not know your thoughts from inside your mind; I only read your face. It is much the way I would know you are happy by seeing your smile.

"And now you wonder why I do not go about the healing immediately." Again the smile. "This healing is a thing of power, and I must first gather my power.

"Also, there is the problem of your people outside. Many of them fear me, some of them doubt my power, and those doubts I must overcome as well."

She sat down cross-legged beside him. "How would it be if, to pass the time, I tell you some stories? There are tales I can tell which I doubt have made their way into the world of men as yet."

So she told him the tale of the Great City of Mathlabbin, how it was founded in ages past, and built, and grew great, and was filled with wonders. The City had towers of crystal and silver and white marble and was fair to see. Yet through jealousy and envy, a war came about.

That war was fought not merely with weapons such as swords and shields, but with magical weapons, weapons of fire and destruction and fear.

At the end of the war, the City was entirely cast down, destroyed with the weapons of magic. And in the end, such was the terror and fear that had been loosed that when the war was ended, none could live in the City any longer. A miasma of fear lay over the City, so that only the hardiest could stay there for any time, and often even they were driven insane by the experience.

It was said that even now there was a feeling of ill-will lying over the ruins of the city, enough to make a person uneasy if they came too close. And there were uncouth and dangerous creatures making their homes in those ruins, so that travel there was dangerous.

She told him also the tale of Dys-Hanglorilar, bearer of the Shield Set in Onyx, who was the Champion of several Kings in succession, and who led armies on their behalf. He was always victorious on the field, and it was said that the sight of the Shield was worth a thousand warriors on his side.

But the day came that King Ofrandith ignored the signs of preparing war for too long, and was only on the point of gathering his own forces when an army of goblins descended on the kingdom. Dys-Hanglorilar set out with a small force to delay them while the King readied his army. The hero met and fought the goblins in the White Mountain Pass, and held them for three vital days.

In the end, goblin arrows and goblin swords cut down their numbers until they were surrounded and completely destroyed. The King, however, had managed to gather his army, and dealt the goblins a bitter defeat. It was said, though, that the White Pass was ever afterward haunted, and that the pass was not a good place to be after nightfall.

With, these tales and many others, she whiled away the time until the evening. From somewhere, she produced an oil lamp and lit it.

"I need no light to do my work, but you would doubtless be more comfortable if you can see what is happening."

She made a sign, and thunder began to sound, low and menacing, but as though it were in the tent with them. Krinneth swore he could hear the sound of voices speaking and even shouting in and around the sound of the thunder, but he could make out no words.

"Now," she said, "the time comes for the real work, and time for the pain I promised you. Here, bite on this." She put a stick of wood between his teeth.

She began to sing, a rising, falling, rhythmic chant. The words of the chant were in no language he had ever heard before. Soon, he was no longer able to pay much attention to the chant, or to anything else. The pain he had suffered previously had been bad, but this was worse, much worse. The pain did not die away if he lay still, as it had done before, but continued to increase.

The thunder within the hut continued, and the sound of words as well, the noise growing louder and louder. Lithlannon's chant wove in and around the other noise, and the rhythm of the words brought an intensity to his pain that he could never have imagined.

At first he bit on the stick, his teeth sinking deep into the wood, but the pain did not go away. The chant rose and fell, and the pain intensified. He thought once to spit the stick out of his mouth and ask her to stop, but when he was rid of the stick, he could form no words. He could only scream wordlessly, on and on, until at last he lost consciousness.

Even then, he was still aware of the pain going on and on, though the pain no longer seemed to touch him.

Suddenly, there was silence all around him. The pain was gone. His clothing was soaked with sweat and he felt weak, as though he had done a day's work and more.

Lithlannon was looking at him over the flickering oil lamp, "I did tell you that there would be pain."

"And I ignored your words, thinking nothing could be worse than the pain I was already suffering." His throat was hoarse, but the most surprising thing he noticed was that the pain was gone.

"Here, drink this. It will help your throat."

"What is it?"

She grinned. "You have allowed yourself to undergo my spells to your great agony, and now you suddenly doubt what I might give you to drink? It is nothing but what you might get from the juice of apples and other fruit, and it will soothe your throat."

He tried to sit up, and was surprised again at how weak he was. She put an arm under him and lifted him, and he was surprised once more, this time at the strength in her. He drank and lay back again.

"So," he said with a small smile, "You have earned my services for nine years. From my present state, I would say that you did not get much of a bargain."

She returned his smile. "Oh, I think that I will be satisfied."

"Is my nine years to begin today?"

Lithlannon tilted her head slightly to one side. "Is there a reason why it ought not to?"

"Clearly, and holding by the letter of the agreement, there is no reason. And if you insist it be so, I will hold by your decision. Yet in my haste, I made an agreement without the permission of he to whom my service is presently sworn. I did so in the full expectation that he would also agree, yet I did so without his specific agreement.

"All I ask is time to go to him and speak to him, to tell him of the circumstances, and beg his permission to leave for nine years."

"And if he will not give his permission?"

He shrugged, not very effectively because of the stretcher on which he still lay. "In truth, in very truth, Lady, I do not know what I should do then."

She looked at him, musing, and said nothing for a time. When she spoke, it was with a smile. "I wonder if I would have felt worse about my bargain if you had not tried to amend it in this manner and for this purpose? So. Do you go and do your business, seek your permissions, and arrange what must be arranged, and meet me here once again in one month's time, at which time you will begin your service.

"And further, every three years for a period of three days, you will be allowed to return home to assure your people that you are not dead."

"Agreed. Will you have me swear any oath that I will return?"

"No. If you will not return, any oath would be only so much wasted breath, and if you will return, then the oath is not needed. But I do have a suggestion for you."

"And what is that?"

"That you lie back and sleep. There are still a few hours until dawn, when you must walk out of here, and you still need rest."

"What of you? Did not all that sound and thunder weary you?"

She laughed. "The sound and thunder was mostly for the benefit of your friends outside. I was sure that at some time you would lose the stick from between your teeth, and there are men in your party who would dare anything if they heard you screaming. I did not want to be disturbed, so thus I produced the noise.

"And to answer your question properly, I have been resting for some time while you were still unconscious, and I will rest again while you sleep. Have no concern for me, but for yourself."

So Krinneth lay back and closed his eyes. It seemed no time at all before Lithlannon was shaking him gently by the arm. He woke, remembered everything that had passed, then rose, amazed at the absence of the pain. He looked around, then picked up the stretcher on which he had lain; the two men would want their spears back. He looked at Lithlannon again, said, "Until next month," and stepped out into the sunlight.

Chapter Four
RETURN TO WESTERMOOR

Krinneth rode back toward the Westermoor. It had not, he reflected, been a very pleasant month. The men who had accompanied them to the Westermoor had been wary of him, as though the magic out of Faerie might have changed him into something beyond their ken.

Worse still was what he had heard from Gwathlinn as they rode back to Dhahal's holding. She herself was nervous about just what might have happened to him, but after a bit of irrelevant conversation, she finally decided he was much the same as ever. He had been watching the countryside round as they rode, noting landmarks in order to find his way back in a month's time. He had also been wondering somewhat about the service he would have to undergo, and what it might comprise.

He had suddenly realized Gwathlinn was talking about their impending wedding. He had turned to her.

"It is perhaps a little soon to be talking of marriage, Gwathlinn."

Her shocked eyes met his. "But I thought that had been already settled between my father and you!"

"Yes, it had. But that was before my wound, before I had agreed to serve the Lady of the Westermoor for nine years in return for my healing. She has granted me a month's leave to make arrangements with your father and all. And I wonder if your father will be so willing to agree to the marriage if I must be gone for nine years."

"You do not really intend to go back to her?"

"I made a promise, Gwathlinn." He thought to mention the agreed visits every three years, but felt it would not help matters.

"A promise? What does a promise count to such a one as that?"

"A promise is a promise, no matter to whom it is given."

She started to argue, then restrained herself. Their conversation, however, was strained for the rest of the journey.

Dhahal had greeted them with gladness, and was openly happy to see Krinneth riding upright in his saddle. When Krinneth told him of the bargain made for his healing, however, his face became grave. Behind that bald forehead, thoughts were going found and round, almost visible to Krinneth.

"I can understand, My Lord, if you no longer consider the agreement we made to be workable," he said.

"No, no, not so hasty now, lad. Look you, this is important news, and I shall have to think on it before making a quick decision. However, it goes, I am happy to have you back, and whole."

However, matters did not improve altogether. Word of what had happened to Krinneth passed throughout the castle with added embellishments at each telling, so that practically everyone was watching him to see how he had been changed, and any slightest thing was seized upon to show that he was not the same man he had been. And if he were not the same man, what was he?

Nor had Gwathlinn given up hope of convincing him to change his mind. She merely switched her tactics. Rather than argue with him, she made herself agreeable, so agreeable that he should certainly have changed his mind and broken his promise to Lithlannon if Gwathlinn and her happiness were all that counted.

Krinneth had seen what she was trying to do, but for the sake of keeping peace, had said nothing to her.

During the last week, however, Dhahal had finally taken him aside to speak to him. "You plan to be away at the end of the week, then?"

"Yes, My Lord."

Dhahal grimaced. He was quiet for a bit, then he spoke. "Look you, lad, do not be thinking I am angry. You did what you thought best, and I take it kindly that you came to ask my leave before you went. And yet there is Gwathlinn. She even wants me to order you not to go."

"And will you do so, My Lord?"

"Perhaps I might, if I thought it would be more than wasted breath. But I understand you, lad. You have given your word, and you will not go back on it. I wish it could have been some other way, but it cannot, and I must be satisfied with that. After your nine years, if I still live, there will be a place here with me."

"Thank you, My Lord."

Gwathlinn had carefully said nothing until the day before the month was up. She had been patient for so long, and could not be patient any longer. "Have you spoken to my father about us yet?"

Krinneth had been expecting this, and he sighed. "Yes, I have spoken to your father. There was little to be said, though, for I must go back to the Westermoor tomorrow."

"You will persist in this foolishness, then?" Her eyes were blazing.

"I made a promise. Lithlannon will be waiting."

"Lithlannon, is it? So familiar, and on such a brief acquaintance? But you were alone together for the whole night in that hut, were you not?"

"Gwathlinn, you insult me."

"I insult you? I had thought you wished to marry me."

"I do." Even while he spoke, Krinneth knew whatever he said would only make matters worse.

"You wish to marry me, yet tomorrow you will rush off to her, to serve her for nine years. And what of me? I should merely wait quietly for you, living here as a spinster in my father's house, waiting on your memory? And if you never come back, then what?" She whirled and stormed away, leaving him standing.

In the morning he had gone to the kitchen to get provisions for his journey, trying hard to ignore the fact that the cooks and scullions all crossed their fingers as they served him, to ward off the bad luck which must be associated with a man charmed into servitude to a being out of Faerie.

Dhahal met him outside the kitchen door. "Surely you did not intend to leave without saying farewell, lad?"

"No, I had intended to come up to speak to you now."

"So I have merely saved you the trouble of seeking me out? Good, good. Come walk with me a moment."

They had walked for some time, going up onto the battlements and walking around. Dhahal was silent, and Krinneth wondered if he would ever speak. And while he was wondering, he looked out over the familiar sights and wondered if he would ever see them again.

Finally Dhahal spoke. "Look you, lad, I will not say that I am happy you are going away. I am not. And I will not deny that I am less happy at the way you are going. But for the reasons, well, if you were one who would break his word, I am not certain that I would want you to stay."

He was quiet for a little longer.

"Look you, there is a place for you among my warriors when you come back. I cannot promise you the same place I offered you a while back; someone must eventually be sent to Garkeep. But if you come back here, I will not drive you out."

"Thank you, My Lord."

"You thank me because I promise to do what is barely right and decent? Lad, I wish I could do more."

"There is no need to do more, My Lord. Just so that I know that I go with your good will."

"You do. And may you come back safely." The older man reached out and drew Krinneth into a crushing embrace, then let him go, looking at him fiercely. "Look you, lad, take care of yourself!"

"I will."

Gwathlinn was not among those to see him off.

Now, approaching the mere itself, he wondered at what he was doing. Strange things were said about Faerie, about those who dwelt within. She had asked for nine years of service from him; was this perhaps merely a way of getting him to come into Faerie, so he could be slain at leisure?

Even as that thought entered his mind, he smiled at the foolishness of it. Had she intended harm to him, she had him at her mercy for most of a night. And with the sort of power she had displayed, it was not a matter of being wary of the retinue which had come with Gwathlinn.

And by the same token, what service of his could be worthwhile to her? He was a fighting man, with the skills of a fighting man. Of magic, he knew nothing. Once when an illness kept him to his bed for a time, he had learned to read and write the common runes, something not many other men of his age and station could say, but he was certainly no spell-caster.

So what could she want?

Over beyond the mere were the dark hills and green forests of Faerie. This was his destination, and all he knew of it were the usual tales and legends of that mysterious land. He knew also that strange and sometimes terrible things occasionally came out of that land as well, and if such made their homes there, what else might he expect?

He rode out toward the mere. The rough hut which had been built for the healing was still standing, though one corner of it was leaning where one of the poles had begun to fall. He looked around. Willows surrounded them, some so near as to hang over the water's edge. A fine place for an ambush, if anyone should have such an intention.

He smiled at that. Well, he had been born and brought up as a warrior, and what else did a warrior learn but fighting, tactics, and the like?

"Now am I to toss in some more goldenrod to summon her once more?" he wondered. The first time, the owlet had met them on the way and given them instructions. This time, he had none. He had seen an occasional owl sleeping in a tree, but that meant little.

Something moving on the far side of the mere. Yes, it was someone on a horse, and from what he could make out, it was Lithlannon. He waited for her.

Around the mere was a path, and the path wound in and out through the willows so that she herself went in and out of sight, appearing and disappearing amidst the branches and greenery. She wore a simple white dress, with a dark green cloak over it. Her long black hair still hung loose and free, down to her waist. The horse she rode was a large black stallion.

Finally, she was near enough so her face was visible to him, and she was smiling. "A good day to you, Krinneth, son of Darun."

"And a good day to you as well, Lithlannon—-" he stopped, realizing he did not know her full name.

She laughed lightly. "You may call me Lithlannon. My full name is Lithlannon Darhinnial, and my titles would be meaningless to you. You are ready to go?"

Krinneth surveyed the land he was leaving. There was a slight movement in the willows. Light reflected on something. He turned to Lithlannon and shouted, "Ambush! Beware!"

Her horse started and reared, turning. Something went past with a "zip", and even as he was moving, he realized it was a crossbow quarrel.

He urged his horse toward the willows. Only one person seemed to be in the ambush, and if that were so, he would have a moment or two before the ambusher could recock his crossbow. In two jumps his horse was in front of the bush, and Krinneth could see the man within, recognizing with a shock the arms of Dhahal on his surcoat.

There was no way to get into the willow bunch on horseback, so he jumped down and sprang forward, sword out. The ambusher had given up trying to cock the crossbow and was pulling out his own sword, but he had barely got it free of the scabbard before Krinneth had thrust him through the chest. He went down.

Krinneth kicked the man's sword out of his reach and knelt beside him. Crossbowmen and mounted knights had few dealings with each other, so that all he could say for certain was that this was one of Dhahal's men. He still lived, but just barely.

"Dhahal sent you?"

"No, not Dhahal. She sent me. Kill the Witch and set you free from the spell. Only-—Too quick-—missed by inches-—curse too strong..."

Krinneth had just opened his mouth to say that there was no curse when he realized the fellow was dead. He wiped off his sword, got up, and looked around.

Lithlannon had ridden over to the edge of the bush and was looking in at them. "Who is it? Someone sent by your lord?"

"No, he said not. He said that he was sent by Gwathlinn, by the lady to whom I had been betrothed. She thought I was cursed, and that to kill you would remove the curse."

"Your people think you are cursed?"

He turned to her and shrugged. "Most think that at the very least, it is bad luck to be too near to me now."

"And what do you think?"

"I?" He realized he had not thought much about it at all. He considered. "Yes, I suppose one might say that bad luck attends me. But the bad luck is mostly the fact that others fear what has been done to me. And I do not think that the fear would be any the less, no matter what might happen to you."

She smiled. "I appear to have chosen wisely. You have at least the beginning of wisdom. You do not blame me, then?"

"Blame you? No, lady, I do not blame you. For if it was not my notion to come to you for healing, at the very least I consented to that healing. If there is blame to be apportioned, I deserve as much of it as any."

She gave him a long, measuring glance. "Good," she said, "you do not harbour ill-will against me. We two will have to work together, and that would be difficult if you hated me as well. Do you wish to bury him?"

Krinneth inspected the sprawled corpse. "No," he said. "They sent him to kill from ambush. Let them come and bury him."

Chapter Five
INTO FAERIE

It might be any stretch of wooded hill country, Krinneth reflected. The trees were trees, huge old oak and ash and willows in bunches, low thorn bushes blocking the way between them except for certain set paths. Such tracks as he observed belonged to deer and rabbits, with the occasional wolf and bear, and the birds were completely ordinary as well, robins, jays, hawks, and the like.

He was suddenly aware of Lithlannon looking at him and smiling.

"It shows so much, then?"

"Only that you seem to expect everything to be unusual."

"And nothing is. Am I wrong?"

"Oh no. Here, on the edges, Faerie and the world outside are mostly quite similar."

"So. And does everyone who comes into Faerie for the first time act the same?"

"Why, as to that, there are so few people who come into Faerie from outside that it is difficult to set a rule and a standard. I expect that it is so, though. It is only natural, after all; you have heard tales of the strange and terrible things that abound within this land, so when you come in, you look for them."

It was at that moment he caught sight of a gryphon sitting quietly in a clearing, warming itself in the sunshine. The bird-head turned toward them, the deep dark eyes regarded them, but the great gold-red beast moved not a feather.

Krinneth looked at Lithlannon. Mirth was in her voice and she was near to laughing as she said, "I said 'mostly quite similar.' There are a few unusual things to be seen."

"I expect I shall get used to it."

"In time, I expect you shall."

They rode in silence for a time, then Krinneth asked, "What will you need me for? How am I to serve you?"

"Ah, there is always a task for a bold man, for one who knows war and weapons."

"I am familiar with swords and spears and what-not. What need have you of them, with the magic at your disposal?"

She laughed. "Ah, that is precisely the difficulty. The magic is not always at our disposal. In fact, it is comparatively rarely that magic can be used, for this cause or that. And it is then that matters come to the strength of arm and heart, and it is then that such as you are invaluable."

He nodded. "So, then. What tasks have you for me to do?"

"Ah, there are many tasks for you to do, but it will seldom be for me to say which tasks you should undertake. I speak with those who rule, but I, myself, am not one of them, and there may be things which they feel are important that should be done immediately.

"But do not fear; no one will send you out at once on a task that is beyond your capabilities. We shall test you carefully first."

Again, they rode in silence for a while. Again, it was Krinneth who broke that silence. "Can you tell me our destination?"

"We are going to Arlith-ysterven, chief of the Elven cities. As I told you, though I speak with those who rule, I am not one of them. It may be that even the King of the Elves will wish to speak to you."

"And what sort of place is this Arlith-ysterven?"

"It is a place of beauty. The Elves built most of it for beauty, of marble and other fine material. There was a time when it had no need of walls, but in these days there is no safety to be found, not even deep in the Elven Realm. There is a wall about it, a great stone wall, with towers and turrets, so that none can come upon it unawares, and none can take the city unless they storm the walls."

"And who are your enemies?"

"They are many, yet they are directed and inspired by only a few, chief among whom is Haldorvan, King of the Dark Elves. The Division of the Dark Elves from the Light Elves took place many years ago, when each took a different direction and purpose in life.

"The Light Elves had been a peaceful people whose interests lay with the study of the wood and the wild, the ways and habits of birds and animals, the growing of plants. With the Great Division, however, they have been forced more and more to learn less peaceful arts."

"And I shall fight against this Haldorvan?"

"No, probably not against Haldorvan himself, but possibly against his minions and allies. There are, for instance, Shtavrak, the King of the Goblins and Hoodaldow, Lord of Ogres, both of whom hate the Light Elves and seek every opportunity to do us ill. Or indeed, there may be other tasks entirely found for you to do."

"So. Tell me more of this city."

They rode on and Lithlannon described the city more fully, so that Krinneth could practically envision it in his mind. He suddenly realized he felt more cheerful than he had since the day of his wounding, so long ago. He doubted if it was a spell, but more likely the result of the company.

"When do we arrive?" he asked.

She laughed. "So eager to be there already? Have I described it that well, then?"

He smiled at her in return. "Yes, in part. But also I see that the sun is going down. How much further do we travel today?"

She laughed lightly again. "A practical man! No, we shall not arrive there for several days. In the meantime, we shall soon stop for the night."

"You say that the city has had to build walls. Are we two safe enough, then?"

She shrugged. "I hope so. Unless matters have changed for the worse, on this side of the city we need only fear the more common beasts who wander the wood, most of whom would not attack us. And for those who would attack? Why, I would expect that your sword would be sufficient to ensure us safety."

For two days, they travelled through the wooded hills. As they drew deeper into Faerie, Krinneth began to observe strange things. He saw several unicorns, even another gryphon (or perhaps the same one, he could not tell) and occasional glimpses of strange things which he could not rightly describe. On the third day, they came across Elves, either solitary or in groups, some older and some younger. A few of them recognized Lithlannon and greeted her, but few of them seemed inclined to much conversation.

He noticed the Elves were generally shorter and slenderer than he was himself, and usually had very light blonde hair. Their eyes were grey or light blue, their features were fine, and they moved lightly along the paths.

Towards the end of that day, they met a band of Elves equipped and ready for war. There were twenty of them, all wearing scale-armour and light metal caps, with bows and arrows slung over their shoulders, short swords at their hips, and spears which they often used as walking-staves. The leader wore a torque of gold around his neck, and when the leader saw Lithlannon and Krinneth, he called out a greeting to Lithlannon. It surprised Krinneth to hear that he used the ordinary speech of the outside world.

"Hail, Lithlannon! You have another one with you, I see. Is he as plump and tasty as the others you have brought?"

"Hail, Vohalton. I see you chatter as foolishly as ever." There was a touch of anger in her voice.

"Ah, but if I did not, would I still be Vohalton?"

"I do not know, but even you must admit that remark was on the border of dangerous."

He did not lose his smile. "Lady, if he has been riding with you ever since the edge of the Wood, will he not by now know better than to believe every foolish thing anyone says? And I hope even I would not risk saying anything too dangerous in front of one who does not know us well."

"Even so, Vohalton, be careful that your careless sense of humour does not get you into trouble."

"Trouble? Lady, we go out hunting for the goblins who are said to have been lurking around the outer villages, and you talk of me getting into trouble over a careless jest?"

Even Lithlannon was forced to smile at the remark. "Yes, I suppose you have trouble enough there. What is the news?"

"Only that armed goblins have been seen. The reports differ as to whether there are ten of them or thirty. They have done nothing so far, which is strange for goblins, and we are going out to reinforce the forces already in the outer villages."

"And we are on our way to the city, and we have delayed you long enough. Farewell, Vohalton."

"And fare you well also, Lithlannon." As they went on, Lithlannon glanced at Krinneth.

He glanced back at her. "Yes, there was a moment when he first spoke that I had some doubts. But as he said, we have been travelling together for nearly two days, and I can hardly believe that you mean me harm."

"Good. Vohalton is a good sort, but he has a sense of humour, which is unusual, to say the least."

"Tell me, the Elves. Are they your people?"

"Ah, you have noticed that I do not look like them? As to who are my people, I do not know. I was a foundling, left on the doorstep of the King of the Elves, and none of their wise folk or soothsayers could say anything of me save that I would do the Elves no ill. But they are my people, in the sense that they have adopted me and made me welcome among them.

"I have tried, on occasion, to find out who I am and from whence I came, but it seems that someone or something does not wish me to have that knowledge. I can discover nothing. There are certain races in the world who resemble me physically, but none of them have the kind of magic it would require to deposit a baby at the door of the King of the Elves, and at that unnoticed. So while I still seek for the secret of my origin, I am no longer quite so concerned about it; I must decide for myself what I am, and then be that person."

All Krinneth could do was nod.

Chapter Six
THE KING OF THE ELVES

Quarannon, King of the Elves, sat in a rather plain wooden chair at one end of a large room. Quarannon stood when Krinneth and Lithlannon approached. The King was tall, for an Elf, though still slighter in build than Krinneth, and he wore his hair and beard long. He had the presence of a wise and kind person, and his smile was grave.

"Welcome back, Lithlannon, daughter of the house. And welcome to you as well, Krinneth, son of Darun."

Krinneth bowed. "I thank you for the welcome, Lord."

The King glanced back at Lithlannon. "Ill news, Daughter. But I would suppose from the time of your arrival that you have probably met Vohalton on the road."

"Yes. And I had already explained to Krinneth that we were safe this far in our own realm." She was smiling, but there was little mirth in the smile. "Do you think this is the beginning of a new war?"

"No, I think not yet. Shtavrak is probably not quite ready. I suspect that what he is doing is trying to give us cause for concern, to have our soldiers marching here and there, to show how he can threaten us as easily as he likes. In a year or two, when he has shown that his forces can come deep into our land, when he thinks he has wearied us sufficiently, then he will attack."

"And what will we do?"

The King took his seat again. "Ah, the Council is divided on that. Some say we should do nothing, husband all our resources against the coming war. Others say we should ourselves begin the war immediately.

Still more say we should take a middle way and respond to every incursion into our territory with a punishing raid into theirs."

"And you? What do you say?"

The King smiled slightly. "Ah, Lithlannon! You always come straight to the point, do you not? I myself tend to think of the middle way, but with some modifications. After all, the goblins outnumber us, and we could well wear ourselves out by responding to each move they make."

He looked down at the floor, staring deep into it as though he had read some future there. His expression said that the future was not a good one. Suddenly, his eyes shot up to meet Lithlannon's.

"Shame on you, Lithlannon! You draw me into councils of war while our guest is standing here, weary from the journey! Go, now, find quarters for him! We can speak more after we have dined this evening." But the smile in his eyes belied the scolding tone in his voice.

The quarters they found for Krinneth were in a large barracks, large enough to house fifty men but mostly empty now. By some means, which he could not quite understand, water, both hot and cold, was available in copious quantities from a pair of pipes.

This was a novelty for Krinneth, for whom baths in warm water had been rare occurrences. When water had to be drawn by hand and heated up over wood fires, getting enough warm water for a full bath was a difficulty. Here, it appeared, water was plentiful, and easily heated, and he took advantage of it.

After he had bathed, he discovered that clothing had been laid out for him. The clothing was a trifle snug, but it fit, and the vest had a many-pointed star in silver embroidered on the front.

Shortly afterward, a young elf came to summon him to dinner. The table was substantial, with King Quaranoon at the head. Krinneth himself was seated somewhat down the table from the head, though not quite at the very foot, and he saw Lithlannon was nearer the head of the table, on the far side. There was no possibility of conversing with her, but she gave him a smile, and he smiled back.

The King rose and introduced Krinneth, then named all the people round the table, none of whose names stayed in Krinneth's memory for more than a few moments. Out of politeness, the Elves did most of the conversation in Krinneth's language, though there were some there who obviously did not speak that tongue.

The food was good, and in great quantity, and there was some sort of berry wine which was served along with the meal, a wine which Krinneth found excellent.

Amid that singing, a young messenger hurried into the hall, bearing in his hand what seemed to be a piece of paper. He took it to the King and handed it over, then stood waiting.

The King read the note quickly, then stood. The harper, well aware of what was going on in the audience, immediately ceased playing and singing, and the whole company, looking around to see what had happened, saw that the King was standing. There was silence.

"Your pardon for interrupting the festivities," said the King, "but messenger birds from some of the outer villages have come in. Goblins have raided them, and are taking away slaves."

There was a chatter of excited voices, then the King held up his hand. "I fear I must leave you for a time to deal with this matter. Lithlannon, would you come with me? The rest of you remain here, and the entertainment will continue."

Though the harper continued to sing and play, it was clear none of the company were really paying full attention. Krinneth himself was wondering what this meant. Clearly, it was more serious than a simple raid for gold, silver, or such booty; at least the King seemed to think so.

It was not much longer before a young messenger came to summon Krinneth, coming quietly up beside him and speaking in Krinneth's tongue, but with something of an accent. Krinneth's first thought was that his service was truly about to begin.

The servant led Krinneth to a small room where the King and Lithlannon sat. They both looked up as he came in. "Sit down, Krinneth," the King said. "It appears that you are about to begin your service before any of us were truly ready."

"What is it you wish me to do?"

"I hope you will be able to rescue the slaves from the goblins. In particular, I hope you will be able to rescue the captives before the goblins can get them back to their lairs."

"You speak as though I will be going alone."

"No, not quite alone. Lithlannon will be going with you."

"The two of us? Against a force of goblins of unknown size?"

"If we had people to send, we would send them. Most of our available troops are already going out toward the villages, but they are travelling afoot, and will not be likely to arrive there in time to do anything. I will give you a token to show to whatever troops you come up with; if there is any way you can use them, do so."

Krinneth looked at Lithlannon. "Have you any particular ideas as to how to do this?"

"Not really, save perhaps to lurk on their trail and cut them down with arrows until we can accomplish something against them hand to hand. What of you?"

"Will any of the troops we come up with be able to ride?"

"Probably the greater part of them. Why?"

"How if we were to lead a few horses along with us? We could pick up a few troops to give us a better chance of success. And at the very least, we could travel faster."

"Good, good!" The King was smiling. "You chose well, daughter!"

"Indeed, I did. What supplies will we need?"

Krinneth thought on that. While he was thinking, the King spoke again. "You will leave tonight?"

She shook her head. "Best get some rest first, and leave as early as possible in the morning."

When he met her in the morning, Krinneth saw Lithlannon dressed in sturdy leather trousers, and a light shirt of ring-mail. Even the lightest of ring-mail, he knew, was a considerable weight, yet she wore it without seeming to notice. At her belt, she had a sword, suitable to her weight and height, balanced on the other side by a dagger. She had a light metal helmet slung from her belt as well, and on her back was a bow and quiver of arrows.

His first thought was to ask her if she could actually use those weapons, but even before the question was fully formed, he realized it would be an insult. From what he knew of her, he was sure that Lithlannon would not carry weapons she did not know how to use.

But she had seen him looking at her. "You do not approve? Ah, I can see that you do not! Your women do not carry arms, do they?"

"No, they do not."

"Ah, neither do the women of the Elves, as a general rule. But I am not truly of the Elves, so that the general rules do not hold for me. And after all, have you not seen things sufficiently strange that a woman armed would be hardly surprising?"

He bowed. "You are right, of course. Yet you must pardon me; one does not unlearn the habits of a lifetime overnight."

She chuckled. "Surely not. Now, what of our supplies? Are they ready?"

"Everything appears to be here. There is even a bow for me."

"Ah yes, you have used a bow, but only for hunting, and you consider it not quite right to use it in battle. It is perhaps another habit to unlearn."

He smiled at that. "I suppose. Now, what of the horses?"

They went to the stables, where they found not only the horses they had ridden in on, but another ten as well. Krinneth looked around, but all he could find were short pieces of rope for haltering them. "We will need a longer rope if we are going to lead these all."

She smiled. "No, they will follow me. Wait a moment." She went to each of the horses in turn, looked it closely in the face, murmuring gently. When she was done, she looked at Krinneth. "Now we put the saddles on; if we do come up with warriors to ride them, they will certainly prefer to have saddles."

"What is this, some sort of spell?"

She grinned as she picked up a saddle. "Perhaps, perhaps not. It is a gift I have to talk to beasts. I doubt it is magic, since all I do is convince them to come along, much as you would convince a person to come along with us."

They were just on the point of mounting up when Quarannon himself come out to see them off. "It is a dangerous undertaking, this. Be careful, daughter. Be careful, Krinneth son of Darun. Do what you can, but do not attempt the impossible; if you cannot rescue the captives without serious risk to yourselves, do not try."

"We will be careful," promised Lithlannon, though Krinneth wondered just how careful it was possible to be in a situation where there were two of them, just possibly as many as twelve, against two to four times that many goblins.

"Farewell, Lithlannon, farewell, Krinneth."

"Farewell, my Lord King."

"Farewell, father."

They turned their horses toward the gate, and the ten riderless horses followed behind.

Chapter Seven
ON THE TRACK OF THE GOBLINS

Even travelling quickly, it took a day and a half to reach the first of the outer villages. The folk of the outer villages were perhaps a little shorter and sturdier of build than the Elves of the City, but their hair and eyes were the same, and they spoke the same language.

On the trip Krinneth had gotten Lithlannon to begin teaching him the Elvish speech. At present, he was not capable of doing more than passing greetings and asking for food and water. Lithlannon questioned the villagers and passed along to Krinneth such answers as were important to their quest.

"This village has seen or heard no goblins, but they say that smoke has been seen in the air at about a day's travel ahead, where there is another village. Some twenty Elvish warriors passed through here a while ago, and they may well have been at the village when the goblins attacked."

"Then if we are planning to catch up to the goblins, we had better ride."

"Exactly."

When they arrived at the next village, they found that something had indeed attacked it. Most of the buildings had been burned, and many of the people killed. Those who were left were still in a state of stunned confusion, wandering aimlessly amid the desolation, peering here and there amid the wreckage left by the goblins.

After a long conversation with an elderly Elf, Lithlannon turned to Krinneth. "There are ten missing, unaccounted for. The tracks where the goblins left are rather muddled and trampled, but there are Elf-tracks among them."

"What of the warriors who were supposed to be here?"

"They had already gone up the trail to the next village along. No one really thought that goblins would attack this deep inside Elvish lands."

"How many were the goblins?"

Lithlannon spoke to the old Elf briefly. "He thinks that they were about thirty. Certainly no more than fifty."

"So. The question now is this: Do we follow after them immediately, or go looking for reinforcements first?"

"A good question. The goblins have something of a start on us, and the longer we wait, the more likely they will get away entirely."

"But they are driving slaves with them. Drive as they will. They cannot march as quickly as usual."

"Then you suggest we look for reinforcements?"

He shook his head. "No, merely considering all we know. I think it best that we two go after them."

"Two of us against fifty?"

"We shall have to think of a stratagem when we come up with them."

"What of the horses?"

"Leave them here. No, on the other hand, bring them with us. At the very least, we can change off horses from time to time, and thus go faster. And we might find some warriors on the trail of the goblins."

"Nor will the people here have time or desire to find fodder for ten horses."

"So let us be off."

At the end of the next day, they knew that they were gaining on the goblins, though they were still far behind. As they rode, in the times when he was not studying the Elvish language with Lithlannon, Krinneth made and rejected plans.

The best plan he could come up with was the one mentioned back before they had left Arlith-ysterven; dog the goblins' footsteps, cutting down their numbers with arrows until it was feasible to attack them hand to hand.

Near the middle of the next day, as they were riding, Lithlannon suddenly gave an exclamation. It was in Elvish, so all Krinneth could do was look at her. She looked at him and smiled. "Elves! Elves on the trail of the goblins, about eight of them, I would say."

"Ha! How far ahead of us?"

"Half a day, perhaps. Less if we push the horses a little."

"Good news! Of course, ten against fifty is only a minor improvement upon two against fifty, but it is an improvement."

They came upon the Elves late that same day, as long twilight shadows turned the forest into a dark and mysterious place. Lithlannon had just said, "We shall have to stop soon; there is scarce light left to see the tracks," when a voice spoke out of the darkness beside the road.

The voice was speaking Elvish, but Krinneth could make out most of the words and guess at the rest.

"Stop! Who are you, and where do you go?"

They held their horses, and Lithlannon spoke a quick sentence which appeared to mean "Business of the King!"

The voice said "Ah, Lithlannon!" Then, with hardly a sound from the bushes, an Elf stepped into the trail, followed by several others. They were all armed, and all had arrows on their bowstrings. The leader spoke again to Lithlannon, and Krinneth understood nothing of this at all.

Lithlannon spoke in answer. "Hail, Holvannon! In politeness to my companion, please speak the language of men. He is learning Elvish, but has hardly had time to become proficient."

Holvannon cast a glance toward Krinneth, and there was not much hospitality in the look. "Seldom have our two peoples met without ill coming of it! You brought him here, Lithlannon?"

"I brought him here, Holvannon, because it seemed good to me to do so. And he is presently coming with me to help try to rescue our people from being taken as slaves by the goblins. If you cannot at least be polite to an ally, then be silent."

Holvannon looked down for a moment, then looked back up. He made no apology, and it was clear that he would make none. "You will join us, then?"

"Even better, we have horses for all, so that we can make better time."

"Good! Did you plan to ride through the night?"

"No, it is already becoming too dark. Let us camp for the night and be up by first light."

"Will the goblins allow us to be so leisurely with our time?"

"The goblins will allow it. They are out for slaves, after all, and though the goblins themselves are hardy enough to march throughout the night and the day as well, most of their captives are not. They must rest some time."

Holvannon nodded, but he was clearly not altogether convinced. Later on, as they sat round a small fire eating their evening meal, Lithlannon asked Holvannon, "How do you come to be following the goblins?"

"We were well up the road and we saw the smoke. We went back to the next village, expecting that the goblins would come through there before they started for home. I fear we waited too long before we realized that they were not coming."

Lithlannon nodded. "Well, we ought to come up with them tomorrow, unless perhaps they suspect that we are on their trail, and abandon their captives to move faster."

"And if they abandon their captives, you know that they will not simply leave them behind?"

"No, they will probably kill them. And that means that we must catch them before they know that we are near."

By the next afternoon, it became clear from the sign that they were rapidly overtaking the band of goblins. "The captives are slowing them down even more than I had expected," Lithlannon said.

"And now is the time to decide what we are to do," said Krinneth. "Ten of us are still too few for an outright attack on this many goblins."

"Quite so. Therefore, I have a plan to suggest." She outlined her plan, and when she had finished, both Krinneth and Holvannon spoke vehemently in one word.

"No!"

She smiled at them. "I am encouraged to see the two of you in agreement about something. However, I do not think there is a real alternative."

"But the risk, Lithlannon! If you die, how can I go back to your father and tell him that I allowed you to go thus to your death?"

"In the same way you would tell him of the death of any other Elf in your company, I imagine. But there are a few other things to be considered here. For instance, we are quite near to Derdrona, the Mountain of Ill Luck, which is the destination of the goblins, and once they are inside, I doubt we could bring them out. And second, hanging on their heels and picking them off requires more time than we have. And third," Her eyes narrowed as she stared grimly at Holvannon, "I am in charge, as I have said, and I have the King's permission to take under my command such warriors as I meet. That being said, unless you can tell me immediately of a better idea, we will follow my strategy."

Chapter Eight
BENEATH THE MOUNTAIN

Krinneth sat high in a tree, feeling very uncomfortable and rather vulnerable. He was assured by the Elves that he could not be seen, and further assured that the goblins would not be looking up at the trees, at least not until it was too late. The Elves themselves were also hidden in the trees around him, aside from one assigned to keep the horses from straying. That was something remarkable; a force of humans would have required at least two for that task, possibly three.

He looked around carefully. There was no sign of the Elves. He had watched them climb into the trees. He knew which trees they were in, but they were invisible. It was one attribute of the Elves, to hide quickly and easily, even where there was little or no cover. They assured him that it was nothing magical, but it bothered him nevertheless.

He thought about Lithlannon, and how she had pushed Holvannon into accepting her plan. She was an interesting person; at one time she would seem a simple, unpretentious maid, at another time a noble lady of the Elves, and again a warrior-maiden and commander of soldiers.

Krinneth knew that among his own people, a woman did not take such a forward role. He had a sense that Lithlannon was not even typical of Elvish woman, though he had not had enough experience to be certain of that.

All this brought him to think again of Gwathlinn; he was not sure what he thought of her. She had brought him to be healed at the mere, brought him against the advice and counsel of many others, and had been proven right. Yet once he was healed, she seemed to have changed;

she had wanted him to break his word to Lithlannon. She had pressed him not to go back to fulfil his bargain, and when he insisted, she had become angry. And he had not quite realized the depth of her wrath until the crossbowman had confessed to having been sent by Gwathlinn.

Why had she changed so? She had cared enough about him to have dared much to see him healed. Why had her love changed?

Suddenly there was a sound from below, and he looked down.

Lithlannon was coming into the clearing. She was wearing a plain white shift and bearing a bundle of plants in her arms. She was singing some sort of song in Elvish, a cheerful little ditty with a rhyming refrain. Lithlannon did not look back, but there was movement in the woods behind her. Krinneth clutched his bow tighter, remembering what she had said about the bow not being considered a proper weapon of war among his people.

Behind her, a small party of about five goblins came into the clearing and then rushed toward her.

This had all been part of the plan; The Elves had ridden hard, by side paths and small tracks in the forest, to reach a point a little ahead of the goblins' direction of march. While Krinneth, Holvannon, and the others had taken their positions in the trees, Lithlannon had gone to wait beside the trail on which the goblins were coming.

When goblins march, they seldom go quietly. She would know well ahead of time when they were approaching, and at that moment she would get up and begin picking plants beside the trail, as though she were merely gathering herbs. As they approached, she would move off into the woods a little, not looking back, and continue her work as though unaware of the approach of the goblins. It was almost certain that they would send a party off to capture her, to add her to the slaves they already had, and she would lead that party deeper into the woods, at last leading them into the ambush.

In this way, the Elves could kill several goblins quickly, cutting down the odds against them when they must finally attack the goblins openly. It would also quite likely unnerve the goblins when their fellows disappeared into the forest and did not return.

It would have been better if she could have drawn off more than five, but that would be enough for now. Carefully, Krinneth put an arrow to his bowstring and waited for the signal.

The goblins were practically hairless, long-armed, stoop-shouldered, with leathery dark-brown skin. Their limbs were heavy and muscular, and their legs were extremely bowed. Their heads were round, with large almond-shaped eyes and large mouths. The goblins' noses varied from the short turned-up variety to huge, bulky beaks.

The five here wore armour which consisted of a jacket of some sort of leather, on which were sewn several plates of metal on the more vulnerable points, and each wore a helmet as well, generally a leather cap with metal plates sewn on it, though one of them had a cap made entirely of iron, with a neck-guard and nose-guard as well. Each of them also wore trousers or kilt of heavy leather.

Each carried a short, thick spear in his hand, a short, heavy sword at the waist, and a round shield with metal rim and metal boss slung on the back on top of a heavy bow and quiver of arrows. Besides that, each of them carried a variety of small daggers, axes, and maces at their belts.

It was difficult to understand how they could believe that Lithlannon had not noticed their presence, but then it was well-known that the ordinary goblin was quite dull-witted, except in matters of warfare and battle.

There was the sound of a piercing whistle, and arrows flew. Krinneth shot once, missed, and shot again, striking one goblin in the chest. The goblin took two more paces, turned, and fell as another arrow hit him in the back. Krinneth was drawing his bow again when he saw the goblins were all down and appeared to be dead.

He returned his arrow to the quiver and climbed down out of the tree. The Elvish warriors were already checking the corpses before he reached ground. He was only jealous for a moment, then he convinced himself that the Elves had certain abilities, which he did not, and lithe quickness of movement was one of them. Lithlannon was looking the scene over, frowning.

"Only five," she said. "I had hoped for ten. It is not good enough."

"Five is five," said Holvannon. "Better five than none at all."

"I wonder if we ought to try this trick again."

"No," said Holvannon. "Goblins are stupid, but not so stupid as to be taken in by the same trick twice in a day."

She shook her head. "You are right. And I fear that having lost even these five will make the others hurry to get to Derdrona. We are going to have to move quickly."

"We have an advantage over the goblins," said Holvannon. "We know these woods much better than they do. They are confined to the main trails; we can take the side trails. And with horses, we can stay with them, shoot from the trees and be away before they can do anything."

"They have bows, too," Krinneth said.

Holvannon gave him a pitying glance. "And they can see an Elf in the bushes?"

Lithlannon spoke then. "I am afraid we have few choices as to what tactic to employ. We must rescue the slaves before they come to Derdrona. Let us go now. We will work in pairs, and Krinneth shall come with me. Despite the way Holvannon makes this all sound easy, we are likely to lose more than one warrior in this fight.

"Go on now, take your horses and ride."

Thus, they dogged the steps of the goblins through the forest, shooting an arrow or two from cover, then fleeing. After the first few ambushes, they found the goblins going along with bows strung, peering carefully from side to side.

Krinneth, not being so capable of hiding in the brush as the Elves, had to hide somewhat away from the trail in order to flee quickly and easily enough into the trees behind him. Even so, several times as he fled, he felt an arrow come closer to him than he liked.

Krinneth found little time for talking with Lithlannon during this time, but he found out some things. Derdrona was a major fortress of the goblins and was right on the edge of Elvish territory. The Elves had never been happy about the presence of this fortress, but could not remedy the matter.

"There was a raid attempted many years ago. The hero Lethrion Gyl-Farras took a small force and went in. They never came out again. We learned, from various stories that came out, that the goblins were more numerous than Lethrion had expected."

Shortly after that, the goblins were sending up a small party of three to five scouts ahead of the main body to discover any ambushes. Even this did not succeed too well, but they were now coming near to the mountain, and the goblins were still many.

The Elves took to raiding the rear of the column instead of the front. After a short while, a large body of goblins formed at the back of the column, holding the Elves back while the rest hurried on towards Derdrona.

The Elves were contemplating an all-out attack on the goblins, trying to break through and rescue as many prisoners as they could, when another party of Elves joined them. There were about twenty of them, and they had been in other parties when they had heard the news about the slave raids. They had ridden as quickly as they could, judging that their best move would be to place themselves between the goblins and their destination. Even riding as hard as they could, they were too late for that. But they were in time to join with Lithlannon and her party.

Lithlannon looked around. "So. With this many of us, I think we can make an attack. Are you ready?"

She directed the question to those who had just joined them.

An older Elf spoke for them. "Our horses are weary; I think they may have one charge left in them, but if we do not succeed quickly, we will be in serious difficulty."

She nodded. "Well then, by the First Light and the Great Tree, let us go!"

They trotted through the trees. Ahead of them they could see the mountain, and the metal door set in the side of it. They were near, altogether too near; if they did not catch the goblins before they reached that door, then they would fail.

The trees were thinning out now, and the goblins, with less to fear from ambushes, could move faster. The Elves were seen rather sooner than they would have liked, for the alarm went up among the goblin ranks, and some of them formed a line facing backward while the rest continued to drive their chained captives up the mountain slope.

The Elves paused, launched a flight of arrows at long range, and charged. The goblins themselves loosed arrows, and more than one Elf went down before they came to close quarters. But the goblins were themselves attempting to withdraw, and thus were a little less able to stand the Elvish charge. Suddenly, the remnant of them were fleeing up along the track after their comrades, with the Elves mixed in among them, striking and slashing with their bright swords.

Krinneth was in the thick of the fight, and it was in this kind of fighting where a Man could demonstrate his superiority over an Elf or a goblin. Both the latter races were somewhat lighter and smaller than a Man, and a Man could thus land heavier blows, and more deadly.

In the midst of the fight, Lithlannon came near Krinneth and pointed with her shield up toward the mountain. The iron door was open, and a band of goblins was pouring out, some hundreds of them. Lithlannon was shouting something, but Krinneth could hear nothing. Before he could ask her to repeat herself, she had to turn away to fight a goblin leaping up at her with spear in hand.

He guessed what she was saying, though; she wanted them to fight their way through to rescue as many of the prisoners as possible. He pressed on.

Now there was a mixed mob of goblins, Elf-warriors, and chained prisoners, with some of the goblins literally dragging the prisoners on to the doorway. Krinneth pressed on, trying to get to the front, trying to get at those dragging the prisoners in. It was difficult for the surrounding goblins, who were doing their best to keep him back.

With a sudden surge, Krinneth came to the front of the line, barely noticing that he had passed the iron door. He struck down the goblin at the head of the line, struck down two others who leaped in to try to take his place, Krinneth grabbed at the chains himself and stopped the prisoners who, by this time were gasping with weariness, blindly following whoever was pulling at their chains.

Lithlannon was with him now, and Holvannon, and a few others, holding back a rush of goblins. But another rush of goblins, by sheer numbers, pushed them back away from the door. The iron door slammed shut, and a key turned in the lock. They were trapped!

Chapter Nine
A GIFT FROM DERDRONA

There was light from somewhere, Krinneth noticed with surprise, light enough to see with as they were pushed back into a corner beside the door, fighting every step of the way. The footing became treacherous, with objects rolling under foot, or reaching up to catch a leg. He glanced down to see that the floor was covered with old bones, some in the remains of armour.

The goblins drew back suddenly.

A goblin, somewhat larger than the rest, wearing heavy scale armour and bearing a shield and sword, stepped forward. He spoke in the language of men. (Goblins seldom if ever learn Elvish.)

"I am Shathka, son of Gralkor, and you are my prisoners. Lay down your arms, and you will be well-treated."

"You call us prisoners somewhat early," Lithlannon answered, "While we still have weapons in our hands."

"You have weapons, but you cannot escape. The door is shut, and you are on the inside. If you look down and around you, you will see bones. These are the remains of a party of your people who dared come down into our hold some years ago. They found they could not get out either, and the last few of them, including their leader, died where you stand.

"So your choice is to die in that ill-omened spot, or to surrender yourselves."

Lithlannon did not hesitate. "We will not surrender to be the slaves of goblins!"

Shathka sneered. "When there are none of you still able to hold weapons, those who remain will be our prisoners, anyway. And after the fight, we will not feel so kindly disposed toward you. I shall give you a little time to think on that!"

He stepped back to stand among his people, and they all stood glaring at the Elves with fierce yellow eyes, grinning and gnashing their teeth. The Elves waited silently. Some of them had water bottles, which they passed around. None of them took their eyes off the goblins, for to a goblin, breaking a truce was no great matter.

Krinneth considered their situation, but said nothing. It was clear they were doomed; as Shathka had said, for they were too few to fight their way to the doors, even if they had a way to get out. Well, a warrior who died in battle had no real complaint to make; there were worse deaths.

Surrender to the goblins was impossible. He knew what kind of fate awaited slaves of the goblins, knew it from the attitude of the Elves and from what they had said and hinted. A slave of the goblins lived a short life full of hard work, for a slave was only a thing to be worked to death, perhaps eaten after death, and replaced by another slave.

After about an hour had passed, Shathka stepped forward again. "Have you considered my generous offer?"

"Your offer was long ago rejected, Shathka. We will not surrender."

"So be it then," said Shathka with a sneer. "You have had your opportunity and rejected it. Your fate is on your own heads."

He stepped back and signalled, waving his sword over his head, and the goblins charged with a yell. Krinneth was at Lithlannon's side, fighting desperately. No sooner did one goblin fall than another leaped in to take his place.

He suddenly found himself facing a large goblin, almost as tall as he was himself, and broad and heavy to go with it. The goblin wielded a heavy mace in both hands, smashing at Krinneth for all the world like a smith hammering out a sword-blade. Two times, three times,

Krinneth parried the blows by slipping them off his sword. The fourth blow caught his sword just a little too squarely, and the blade shattered.

Jumping back, weaponless, to avoid the next blow, Krinneth caught his heel on something and went down. He saw Lithlannon step in to engage the goblin before he could bring his mace down and finish his fallen opponent, while Krinneth looked around for something, anything, to use as a weapon.

Amid the Elvish bones was a skeleton on its back, arms flung out, and near the outstretched right hand was the handle of a flail. The flail was not a weapon he was particularly skilled with, but it was better than nothing.

He muttered, "With your permission," to the skeleton, then took up the flail and surged to his feet.

He had not thought to have struck so hard, but the large mace-wielding goblin went down at the first blow. Others stepped in, but Krinneth continued to strike with the flail, and with each blow, a goblin fell. Suddenly, a wail rose up among them, what seemed to be a single word in the goblin-tongue, repeated over and over.

An instant later, the goblins had fallen back all the way across the cavern, with Shathka haranguing them as they went. Krinneth turned to Lithlannon. "I have no notion what this is all about, but at least we have a breathing space."

Lithlannon was busy at that moment listening to a little man, one of a group of three. They were not Elves, nor were they goblins, for each of them had a full head of hair and a long beard, and they each had a certain lumpy handsomeness which was completely alien to the goblin race. He suddenly realized that these were the Facherlein, the Little Makers, of whom he had heard, even in the world outside.

She turned to Krinneth. "They believe they can open the door, if we can give them a little time."

He shrugged. "Why not? If we are to die, best we should die trying."

She turned and shouted to the rest, warriors and prisoners, then strode forward. Krinneth was at her side as they made for the door.

Shathka and a few hardy goblins rushed forward to stop them, though the bulk of the goblins refused to move. The flail and the bright swords of the Elves held them back, and eventually they withdrew, having lost many of their number.

In the time of rest which they were granted, Krinneth looked at the door and the Facherlein feverishly working away around it. Lithlannon walked over and asked a quick question, which was answered briefly and impatiently by one of the little people. Then she came back to stand by Krinneth. "He says that they never promised it would be easy, and that they are working as hard as they can. He even suggested that I do my business and let him do his."

She smiled to show she did not feel insulted.

"Yes, and I think we shall have to do our business again; Shathka has convinced them to attack once more."

And indeed he had. A combination of personal threats and the threat of what the King of the Goblins would do to them brought the army of goblins surging forward.

Krinneth noticed immediately that most of the goblins had no desire to face him. A few tried to fence with him, a little tentatively, but dropped back when he pressed them. Others actually tried to fight with him, but he could tell their hearts were not in it.

All this gave him plenty of opportunity to help Lithlannon on his left and the Elf on his right, whose name he never discovered.

There was not much time for thinking, but he felt that the goblins' fear was not due to him, but because of the weapon he was using. It also appeared to him that the weapon was more effective than it ought to be, particularly given his indifferent ability with that sort of weapon.

Finally, there was a semicircle around him where no goblin would approach, and in order to fight, he had to step forward to pursue goblins. He had to be wary in this, for though the goblins feared the flail, if his back was exposed, it would not take much boldness at all for one of them to put a knife or a sword into it.

Then there was a grating and groaning noise behind him, and the light increased as the door opened. A cheer, albeit a weak one, came from the Elvish prisoners, and they moved to flee. The warriors brought up the rear, holding back a redoubled rush of goblins. Krinneth was with them, backing carefully to the door, fighting all the way. The doorway was not terribly wide, and for a time Lithlannon, Krinneth and another Elf held it against a press of goblins.

The goblins still did not like to face the flail, but their captives were escaping and the wrath of their King caused them to dare even that dread weapon. Outside the door, the Elves continued a fighting retreat, moving backward as quickly as they could to prevent the goblins from coming up and encircling them.

There was noise and commotion in the rear ranks of the goblins and Krinneth, looking up, saw that the three Facherlein had climbed up the side of the mountain with some wooden poles, and using the poles as levers had sent some boulders crashing and bounding down the slopes into the goblins.

Some of the freed captives had now taken up goblin-weapons and were joining in the battle as they moved back into the wood. Despite this, the goblins' efforts to surround them looked to be eventually successful; there were just not enough Elves.

More boulders came crashing down from the mountain into the goblins. There was a sudden stir in the woods, and then there were more Elves joining the battle, ten, twenty, a hundred! This was more than the morale of the goblins could stand, and they broke and fled. Shathka cursed at them, shouting dreadful threats, but when he saw they could not be turned, he joined them.

The Elves, after driving the goblins back into the mountain, regrouped and came back to Lithlannon, Krinneth, and the freed captives. Their leader was the same Vohalton who had tried to frighten Krinneth when they had met in the forest. He grinned at Lithlannon.

"They sent messages to tell us that there was trouble over in this direction, so we marched as quickly as we could. We saw the track where you had been pursuing them, and we followed at speed. We were just coming up when one of our scouts came flying back to say the iron door had been flung open and a mass of Elves had fled out.

"Hearing that, we came even faster, and apparently were just in time."

"Just in time, Vohalton. Such promptness even excuses your occasional looseness of tongue."

He grinned in answer, and it seemed she had reminded him of something. He turned his grin to Krinneth. "Ah, you have not yet been eaten? Good, good!"

Krinneth grinned back at him. "No, not yet. Not fat enough, they say. I hear they want me as fat as Vohalton's head before they dine off me."

For an instant Vohalton stood in stunned surprise, then he threw back his head and laughed. "Good, good! A score for you, Krinneth! I shall have to keep an eye on you."

Holvannon broke in. "Now, if we have done with all the nonsense, might we move a little further away from the mountain? If any of the goblins recover their courage and discover just how few we are, we could yet be in difficulties."

"Quite right, Holvannon," said Lithlannon. "Let us move. Vohalton, I hope you have at least a little food. Most of us have been travelling very light, and the prisoners have nothing at all."

They began marching immediately, bringing the weary rescued prisoners with them.

Krinneth marched beside Lithlannon, as usual. Also, as usual, they took up the post of danger in the rearguard. When she was certain that everything was going properly, she turned to him.

"You use that weapon well, Krinneth."

He looked at the flail in surprise. "I think it may be something more than a mere weapon. I have never mastered the use of the flail completely, but with this one, I seem almost unable to miss."

"May I look at it?"

He handed the flail over to her, but there was a certain reluctance in him to let it go. She turned the weapon over in her hands, then said, "Grothrion."

"I beg your pardon?"

She looked up at him. "This is Grothrion, the flail which Lethrion wielded, which was lost when he and his army were lost in Derdrona. It was said that some were worried when it was feared that Grothrion had fallen into goblin hands, but now it appears that we need not have worried."

"But why did they not take the weapon as spoil of the battle?"

"You recall Shathka spoke of that ground as 'ill-omened?' I think that when Lethrion and his last warriors turned to fight, they caused such slaughter among the goblins that the goblins consider that ground to be unlucky, and hence would take nothing from it. It is their habit to take the bodies and armour of their defeated enemies to set them up as trophies, but in this case, they did not even do that. They left everything there, left the slain as they had fallen, and never walked upon that ground again."

"This is a magic weapon, then?"

"In a sense. Grothrion is very potent, and it seems that the goblins recognize the weapon and fear it, which makes the flail even more potent against them."

"Had Lethrion any heirs?"

"No, the flail is yours. But do not trust too much in its potency; remember that you took it from the hands of a dead Elf, and that you too can be slain."

"I will remember."

They walked along in silence for a time, then suddenly Krinneth was aware of someone walking behind them. He turned. The three Facherlein were following them. "What are they doing here?" asked Krinneth.

Lithlannon spoke to them in Elvish, and one of them spoke rapidly in return. She turned back to Krinneth. "He says that since we set them free, they will stay with us for a time."

We set *them* free? Was it not the Facherlein who unlocked the door? Something occurred to him. If they had the tools to unlock the door, certainly they had the tools to unfasten their chains and steal away silently in the night. Why did they not?

She spoke to the gnomes again, and their leader answered her at length. She shook her head and turned back to Krinneth. "I am uncertain of all that he said, but he began by saying that the tools were not immediately available because of the Principle of Uncertainty, coupled with the Doctrine of the Three Small and Three Large ones, and after that it became confusing.

"It is said that in the very beginning, when the Little Makers were first made, they were given great curiosity, and the ability to make and build with only their fingers, and to find tools where no one would see a tool. It is entirely possible, you know, that they picked up things from the floor of the cavern to use as tools."

Krinneth, remembering the state of the cavern floor, nodded. "What are their names?"

She talked to them again, then turned back to Krinneth. She pointed to each in turn and said, "This is Landi, this is Gorni, and this is Varti."

Landi seemed to be going slightly bald, but his hair and beard were red. Gorni's hair was jet black, and Varti's was a reddish brown; this seemed to be the major difference between them.

"Pleased to make your acquaintance," said Krinneth in Elvish, and the three of them smiled and answered appropriately.

"I see that it is imperative that I learn Elvish, and quickly."

By the time they reached the first of the outer villages, their food had been gone for some time, and they were quite hungry. The villagers provided them with sufficient supplies to see them to Arlith-ysterven, and they continued their march, leaving some of the wounded in the care of the villagers.

Chapter Ten
OF ELVES, MEN, AND OTHERS

The minstrel was singing, singing one of the old ballads of the old Elven Heroes.

"To windward did the green drake rise
And spread his wings to seek his prey;
And drifted in the silent skies
To search and stoop and slay."

The song was all in Elvish, but Krinneth was now sufficiently versed in the language which he could understand the whole song without asking for a translation.

This particular song he had heard before, for it was something of a favourite of the Elves. It was one of the adventures of Dys-Hanglorilar, The Tale of the Dragon's Tooth, and was often called for at Elven gatherings.

For himself, Krinneth was wondering what he might be called upon to do next. The Elven King had been pleased when they had rescued the slaves from the goblins, but in the three weeks since then, he had given Krinneth no new duties. Krinneth had spent much of that time with Lithlannon, learning the Elvish language. In the process, he had learned much about the Elves as well.

"Do you no longer go to the mere?" he asked once.

"Ah, what of the poor people who come seeking the Maid of the Westermoor? Fear not, there is not one Maid but several. If I am not there, there will be another."

"But why do you go there at all? To recruit warriors, as I was recruited?"

She laughed. "Oh no, that kind of thing happens very seldom, if ever. The whole purpose is to provide healing, and to try to show men they need have no fear of the Elven people. Payment is always required, for who would believe anything but ill of someone who offered free healing?"

"But there are other humans who have come to Faerie, to dwell with the Elves?"

"Oh yes, indeed there are. Most of them are warriors, and most of them came out of love for an Elf-woman. But there are not many of them, perhaps a dozen or so. There are also several human women among us, most of whom also came for love."

Krinneth frowned. "Then why me? Why was I chosen?"

"I do not know. All I know is that when I saw you, it seemed to me that it was necessary to call you from among your own people to live with us. The feeling came to me that you would do great things for our people."

"Great things? Such as what?"

She shrugged. "Such feelings never reveal details, else they would be more than feelings. But have you not already shown promise?"

"Because I picked up the flail of Lethrion Gyl-Farras when it was practically thrust into my hand? You must realize that even that would not have saved us if Vohalton and his Elves had not come up when they did."

"And is it less important because you could not do it without help? First, without the flail, we would never have gotten out of Derdrona alive, for even Vohalton would not have saved us if we had not managed to open the door. The flail is important, and your possession of Grothrion is probably also important, but we shall have to wait to see the manner of its importance."

And as happened from time to time when he was in a musing mood, Krinneth wondered about his future. He remembered how his own people had treated him when it was merely a matter of his having received healing from an Elf, and agreeing to work in Faerie for nine years. What would be their attitude when he came back? Would he be able to live there at all?

He shook himself and brought his mind back to the present. The minstrel was still singing.

"*Three times the hero drew his bow;*
Three times the wooden shafts did fly.
The drake by these was not brought low,
But circled in the sky."

A young Elf approached Krinneth and whispered to him. "The King wishes to speak to you."

Since it had become known that Krinneth was determined to learn to speak Elvish, the Elves had taken to speaking to him in Elvish, unless he asked them to do otherwise.

When he came to the King's quarters, Krinneth found the King waiting there, and on the edge of his table sat a small man, no more than a forearm-length tall, clothed in green from head to foot, with a pair of wings neatly folded on his back. He carried a small sword on his left side, a smaller dagger on the right, and a bow and arrows slung over his back. He was presently drinking the King's wine from a cup not much larger than a thimble.

"Ah, Krinneth! Thank you for coming so promptly. We will wait a few minutes, if you do not mind; there are others coming, and I would find it easier if I did not have to say everything several times over. In any case, let me make some introductions. Krinneth son of Darun, this is Michmesh Flowerbud. Michmesh is of the Puchlein."

Krinneth bowed. "Pleased to make your acquaintance."

The little winged man stood up on the table, looked Krinneth up and down, then made a curious gesture, putting a palm before his face with the first two fingers spread, touching his forehead. He spoke Elvish, with some strange flourishes.

"And I am being pleased to meet you as well. Quarannon has been telling me much about you, for certain, for certain."

Krinneth was a little taken aback at the little man's so casual references to the King of the Elves, but Quarannon himself spoke up, smiling. "The Puchlein have never shown very much regard for any rank outside their own, and not much for that. You must take him as he is, not as you might wish him to be."

Michmesh turned to look at the King of the Elves. "Ah, Quarannon, you would not be sending me off in the company of one of those for whom every word must be having a 'Milord this' or 'Lordship that' as though to be making it smell the sweeter?"

The King's smile broadened. "No, Michmesh, I know better. You would eventually weary of such a one and lead him to the middle of a bog and leave him. I believe Krinneth will deal quite well with you."

"Ah, well, then, if you are promising so, then I will be doing what I am able to not to be making his life miserable, for certain, for certain."

"Excellent. Now, Krinneth, a cup of wine while we wait for the others?"

It was not much longer before Lithlannon came in, followed by Vohalton. "Ah," said Vohalton, "Whenever I see one of the Wee Folk here, it usually means bad news. What is it now? Hordes of goblins marching on us, the ogres massing in armies, Haldorvan up to his tricks?"

Lithlannon said nothing, but looked at the King.

Quarannon looked up. "Both of you are acquainted with Michmesh, are you not? Good, then let us begin. As you well know, Michmesh and his folk have been of occasional service to us, bringing us bits of news they pick up from time to time. No, Vohalton, it is not always bad news, no matter what you say. And I shall let Michmesh tell you what he has told me. Michmesh, if you will be so kind?"

The little man, seeing himself become the center of attention, sat up straight, spread his wings, folded them once more, took a deep breath, and began.

"We of the Puchlein are ever wandering the forests, wandering sometimes where larger folk do not be daring to go. Even we, though, were not daring to go to the Derga-drish-hona, the place of tumbled stone, the place that you do be calling Mathlabbin. And as Quarannon was saying, we are ever bringing news to you from our wanderings.

"So when it was that some of our bolder young folk had been going to Mathlabbin and were describing some of the things that they had been seeing there, we were thinking it best if word were being brought to you.

"Many ogres have been making their homes in the ruins of Mathlabbin. Ogres are usually being dull of wit, large, and strong. They are also being fond of things bright and shiny, and they gather such and will be keeping them forever stored away in their treasure-rooms.

"My folk are being a curious lot, willing to dare much for the sake of satisfying that curiosity. The treasure-rooms of the ogres are being locked and guarded, but there will always be ways of being found to elude the guards and pass the locks. Strange things were being discovered.

"Among other things, the Shield Set with Onyx was being found."

He looked around to see the reaction to this piece of news.

Lithlannon's face showed surprise, Vohalton's showed pure scorn. "The Shield Set with Onyx was lost in the battle of White Mountain Pass, far away from Mathlabbin, and many, many years after the fall of the city."

"The Shield was never found on the battlefield," Quarannon said.

"Because some goblin carted it away as spoil."

"But you know how goblins are. The Shield was too fine, too rich a piece to be allowed to be given to any lowly goblin, even were he the one to find it. It would have been taken by some goblin-chief, and a high-ranking one. And in that case, he would have known well what he had, and would have flaunted it in our faces in any battle over the past hundreds of years.

"But ogres! Ogres often haunt the edges of battlefields, and often will slip in to take away something which strikes their fancy, and may even escape with it. So perhaps some ogre found it and took it away, and hid it in his treasure-room. And it could quite well be that ogre knew just what he had, and told no-one. Ogres rarely tell even their closest companions about the best pieces in their treasure-rooms. Thus it has not come to the attention of Hoodaldow the Ogre Lord, or he would certainly have claimed it by now."

Vohalton spoke again. "Lord King, I can already guess why you have called us here. You believe this story, and on such evidence as this, you are about to send an army to Mathlabbin to recover the Shield Set with Onyx. Am I not correct?"

"No," said the King, "Not an army. An army would be noticed, and too many would wonder why an army might go to Mathlabbin. Rather, I plan to send a very small party, such a party as could creep in and out unnoticed, discover if the shield which the Puchlein have seen is truly the Shield itself, and if so, remove it."

"By the Great Tree! And I suppose I would be quite able to guess just who would make up the small party undertaking this task?"

Quarannon raised his eyebrows. "This is a task which I would not assign to anyone who was unwilling. If you do not wish to go, Vohalton, I could send another in your place. Klitherion, for instance."

"Klitherion! Klitherion! You would send Klitherion to do something more difficult than fetching wood for the fireplace?"

"If you feel it is too difficult to undertake Vohalton, I shall have to find another."

For a moment, Vohalton was speechless. Finally he said, "This is underhanded dealing, Milord Quarannon! You put such choices before me, either go to into near-certain doom, or to be replaced by one we both know to be near useless on such a venture! Yes, I will go."

The King smiled. "Good. I knew I could depend on you. And you, Lithlannon?"

"I will go too."

"And you, Krinneth? Before you answer, let me tell you that this is certain to be a dangerous feat, and that some of you or all of you may not return. And you need not agree to go simply because the two before you have agreed. How say you?"

"I will go." answered Krinneth.

"Good. Lithlannon, take three days to make your preparations. Michmesh will guide you."

When they reached the hall once more, the minstrel had ceased singing, and the three Facherlein were demonstrating a flying machine. It was round, about the size of a wild goose, with long wings made of thin leather stretched over a light framework of rods. The wings, which had somewhat the same shape and size as those of an albatross, pivoted on small metal protrusions which extended out of the side of the body of the machine. A rod coming out of the top of the body caused the wings to move.

"What causes the wings to move?" asked one of those present.

"Ah," said Landi, "It is powered by steam. We light a small fire inside, which heats a tank of water, which sends steam through a series of pipes to cause the mechanism to move."

"Will you make it fly now?"

Landi scratched his head. "Well, we have only just put the machine together, and we have no idea whether it will fly or not. It certainly ought to, from our calculations, but..."

"Try it!" called an Elf. "Let us see if it works!"

Others took up the cry, and the three gnomes were not very difficult to convince. They gathered some very small sticks, opened up the machine, built the small fire, filled up the water tank, then stood by to watch.

For a while, nothing happened. Then a hissing noise began, and steam began leaking from here and there. For a time, there was no further activity. Then Varti stepped forward and gently pumped one of the wings up and down a few times, then stepped back.

The wings continued to flap, first slowly, then with increasing speed. Despite the rapid beating of the wings, the machine did not lift itself from the table. It began to rock slightly as the wings beat faster, and it set a wind up which was felt in the farthest corners of the hall. Still, the machine did not lift from the table, but began to rock more and more until at last it rolled over onto its back. Steam began to hiss out at an alarming rate, and something went 'pop!' A small bit of metal rang against the stone roof, ricocheted off a wall and the floor, then finally landed in the lap of a startled Elf. He brushed it away quickly, shouting as the heat of it stung him.

The wings of the machine suddenly ceased beating, which allowed an equally sudden increase in the clouds of smoke and steam. One of the little men rushed into the cloud with a bucket of water; there was a hissing sound and more steam appeared, though the smoke appeared to have diminished.

Suddenly Varti appeared out of the smoke and steam, standing on one of the tables. There was no sign of embarrassment on his face as he said almost absently, "I beg your pardon, Lords and Ladies, but it appears that our flying machine requires a good deal more work. We shall have to recheck our calculations."

There was a roar of laughter from the assembled company. The gnomes, still completely unembarrassed, began to take the machine to pieces in order to carry it away.

Chapter Eleven
THE JOURNEY TO MATHLABBIN

When Michmesh, Vohalton, Lithlannon, and Krinneth came to the gates of Arlith-ysterven, they found the three Facherlein waiting for them.

"What do you here, friends?" asked Lithlannon.

"We go with you," answered Varti.

"No, we are going on a difficult and dangerous journey. I cannot allow you to join us."

"Ah, but we will come in any case. Can you prevent us from following after you? If you will not allow us to travel with you, then that is what we shall do. So you might as well allow us to come along with you."

"This is a dangerous journey, no simple walk in the woods."

"Twice now you have said it is a dangerous journey, and we believe you. But we have a duty to you as our rescuers, and we will come along. Do you doubt our valour?"

"No, not really. Only perhaps your experience."

"But you know nothing of our experience. How can you doubt what you do not know?"

Lithlannon hesitated. "Well, then, come along." She did not appear pleased at the prospect. "But be careful, and understand that in this quest, there is one leader, and when I say to do something, you will not hesitate, but do it immediately."

The three Facherlein smiled broadly, then Varti spoke. "Agreed, with the one reservation that you will not tell us to go home."

Lithlannon could not suppress a smile. "Agreed."

Michmesh had watched all this with some degree of disgust.

"What will they be doing?" he asked. "They are not being the sort who could be successfully fighting ogres! And if we have to be fighting, we will not be wanting to protect some useless bodies for certain, for certain."

"You heard them, Michmesh. They will come whether we wish it or not. And we hope to avoid fighting, do we not? After all, there are only the three of us, and how many ogres could we fight, we three? And that being so, why not allow them to come along?"

"If you say so, then, but I will not be liking it at all, at all."

When it came time to camp for the evening, the Facherlein demonstrated some of the equipment they had brought along. One thing was a fire-starter in which a spring drove a metal hammer against a piece of flint, which flung sparks onto a bit of dry tinder. This item worked quite well, but they had less luck with their tent.

The tent should have required no tent-poles. As Varti explained it, the tent consisted of two thicknesses of canvas, stitched together at various points throughout, and sewn tightly around the outside seam. They would blow air into the seam, much as one fills up the bag of a bagpipe, and the shape of the cloth, the larger outer layer attached to the smaller inner layer, would cause the cloth to stiffen up into a large round bubble.

There was a difficulty, however. Each of them blew into the seam until they were worn out with blowing, and still the seam did not fill up. Without embarrassment, Varti suggested to the other two that they should find some sticks to prop the tent up for the night. Turning to the rest of the party, he said, "The air is leaking out as we blow in. We shall have to try to find where the hole is, but that can be done later."

TWO DAYS OUT OF ARLITH-ysterven, the party came upon a gryphon. Ordinarily, the gryphon is a shy beast, avoiding men, and fleeing when it hears the first sound of them.

On this occasion, however, the party had come quietly into a clearing in the wood, and were halfway through the clearing before they realized the beast's presence. The gryphon had been sleeping soundly, and it noticed them at about the same time as they first noticed it. A gryphon needs a short run before it can begin flying, and the party were in front of it, blocking its way. A little distance behind the gryphon, overhanging willows would prevent it from flying.

The gryphone was on its feet in an instant, black bird-eyes flashing at them. It gave a scream like an eagle, turned and trotted toward the willows. Under the willows, it turned again and raced toward them. Michmesh had a small arrow on his bowstring already, but Lithlannon put a hand on his shoulder. "No, wait!"

Krinneth had Grothrion out of his belt and saw that Vohalton had his spear presented toward the beast. The gryphon screamed again and sprang. Krinneth drew back his hand for a blow, and in that same instant the gryphon spread its wings; a tawny shadow passed just over their heads, and with a final scream, the beast was gone into the sky, massive wings taking it rapidly up and up.

Krinneth and Vohalton looked at each other, and Krinneth saw Vohalton was sighing, then noticed that he was doing the same, and smiled. The three Facherlein, at the rear of the party, had dropped all their bags and baggage and were making ready to use short heavy spears, and they seemed quite grateful to put these aside.

As the party continued on its journey, Krinneth spoke quietly to Lithlannon. "I saw the Puchlein ready his bow when the gryphon looked about to attack. Just as well you restrained him; such an arrow could have done little more than enrage the beast."

She smiled at him, a smile of gentle mockery. "You really know little of the Puchlein, do you? They brew a very powerful poison from certain plants, and they dip the tips of their arrows in this poison. If Michmesh had shot, the gryphon would likely have been dead within twenty or thirty heartbeats. But you are partly right; the wound would have enraged it, and a full-grown gryphon such as that can do considerable damage in twenty or thirty heartbeats."

He grinned back at her. "Just as I feel I have learned enough to survive, some other strange thing happens. Remind me I ought not to anger one of the Puchlein."

Other than that incident, most of the journey to Mathlabbin was uneventful. At last, there came a day when Michmesh talked to them in the evening, giving them a warning. "From this time on, we must all be going as softly and quietly as the Puchlein. We will be approaching the first of the fallen stones of the city tomorrow. There are being many dread things within the city, for certain, for certain. If one of them will be attacking us, others may be coming to steal the prey, or to help finish it off, or simply to watch. Thus, we will not be wishing to attract attention to ourselves at all, at all. You are all understanding?"

Everyone nodded.

The next day found them walking on a trail which was clearly all that remained of an ancient road. The woods and the undergrowth had come back so strongly, however, that in most places it was a mere footpath, and only here and there were the signs of the wider road it had once been. In the afternoon, the Puchlein stopped them and pointed out the city, directly ahead.

Only after he had pointed it out could they distinguish the fallen blocks of stone and tumbled columns. The forest had come back here as well, and moss and creeping vines masked the sharp edges of dressed stone. Two tall columns still stood directly in front of them, and Lithlannon asked, "Is this the Great Gateway, the entrance to the city?"

The little man gave a little shrug. "The old roadway does be leading directly between the two standing stones. However, just within the gateway is lying a nest of beasts, being as hungry as they are ugly, and we will not be going in that way."

The way he led them in lay right across the fallen wall, on a pathway that was barely visible through and around the jumble of stone. Except where the trail lay, the rocks were slippery with green moss, and whenever any of the three Facherlein stepped off the trail, they slipped and nearly fell, and Michmesh would turn and glare at them.

"Enough noise you are making," he would whisper savagely, "to tell every beast and ogre in the city that we are coming!" Krinneth himself was concentrating on watching his own footing. His feet were larger than those of anyone else in the party, and he had never been trained to slip quietly and cautiously into an enemy camp. Like all the others, he walked with an arrow to his bowstring, and like all the others, he hoped that it would not be needed.

They were going along with Michmesh leading, followed by Lithlannon and Krinneth, then the three Facherlein, then Vohalton taking up the rear. The three gnomes were taking this very seriously, walking along holding their short broad-bladed spears at the ready, and peering cautiously from side to side.

The trail led past two huge stone slabs which had fallen together to form a triangular opening, about half again the height of a man, and ten paces deep. There was a whiff of carrion about the place, and Michmesh signalled for them to come rapidly but quietly.

Krinneth had just passed by when he heard a squawk from one of the Little Makers behind him. He half-turned to signal for silence and discovered the reason for the noise. Out of the opening was coming a monster.

Though no giant, when the monster stood upright, it was an arm's length taller than Krinneth. The monster was man-shaped, save for two heads, and each of the heads had the same rounded shape and the same features as that of a goblin, save that each of them was topped by a thatch of black hair. It wore a sort of shirt made of some sort of hairy hide, apparently two thicknesses of hide, which hung down just below the hips. It had two long brawny arms, and in each of them the monster carried a spiked club. Though Krinneth had never seen one himself, he recognized it from descriptions he had heard. It was a Dwaghebel.

They were of low intelligence, though they had some degree of shrewd cunning. The two heads could operate independently, and so did each of the two arms. They were normally shy, though if they found a lone man or Elf, they would attack, seeking food. In this case, the party was passing directly in front of the beast's lair, which made him even more inclined to attack.

The first objects of his attack were the Facherlein in front of him, who scattered from his path like chickens under a stooping hawk. Krinneth automatically brought up his bow and loosed his arrow, but the Dwaghebel at that very moment was swinging his left-hand club at Landi, who hopped out of the way with more agility than Krinneth would have expected. The result was that Krinneth's arrow went by just over the Dwaghebel's shoulder.

This, of course, brought Krinneth to the attention of the Dwaghebel, who grinned a double grin and strode toward him. Krinneth loosed another arrow, but in a quick movement, the Dwaghebel knocked the missile out of the air with his right-hand club. Krinneth reached for another arrow, but by the time he touched it, the huge foe was towering over him, swinging back a club to strike.

He dropped his bow, dodged aside, and tried to pull Grothrion from his belt. As he was doing so, a block of stone tilted slightly under his foot, causing him to stumble and fall. As he went down, the club of the Dwaghebel whistled past his head. He rolled away, trying to come to his feet, and saw that the monster was following as quickly as Krinneth was able to move. Then he hit another piece of stone and could roll no further, and the Dwaghebel loomed over him again.

As Krinneth swung Grothrion around to hit the monster's ankle, the only part he could reach, Krinneth saw the Dwaghebel flick up his left-hand club to knock another arrow aside; so that had not been pure luck. On the other hand, Krinneth saw a tiny arrow hanging out of the fur of the shirt. From the look of it, it had not penetrated to the skin, so it would do no good.

The Dwaghebel hopped back out of the way of the swinging flail; Lithlannon leaped in, thrusting with her sword, then leaped back out again before the Dwaghebel could do more than turn slightly in her direction. Krinneth was up now and swung Grothrion at the monster's back. The beast, however, was moving even as Krinneth struck, so the blow was only a glancing one. Despite that, it almost brought the Dwaghebel to his knees. The beast hopped twice to maintain his balance, then turned on Krinneth again. The battle now became hand to hand, with Vohalton, Krinneth, and Lithlannon leaping in to attempt a blow whenever the Dwaghebel turned his back. This was difficult, however, for the beast was quick, and with his two heads and ability to use two arms, he could fight in two directions at once. On the other hand, he was only able to move in one direction at a time, and while he might defend in one direction and attack in another, it was usually possible to tell in which direction he would be moving.

In the meantime, Michmesh hovered here and there, seeking a clear shot. Twice he loosed arrows, only to have the Dwaghebel knock them aside with a flick of his club. The three Little Makers had apparently moved well away from the battle, and were to be seen in a little knot off to one side, with their heads together as though they might wager on the outcome.

Suddenly Vohalton went staggering sidewise, caught by a glancing blow from one of the clubs. The Dwaghebel strode forward to finish him off, and both Lithlannon and Krinneth sprang forward to draw him off.

From behind came a snapping sound as of a heavy bow, and there was a whistling overhead. Out of nowhere, a light but strong cord was wrapping itself around the monster's raised right hand, distracting him just enough for Vohalton to roll aside. Lithlannon struck with her sword, and the Dwaghebel turned toward her, swinging his left-hand club in a backhand stroke which she barely dodged. At the same moment, Krinneth struck, landing a blow with Grothrion square in the chest. The Dwaghebel staggered back and went down.

He was up very quickly, though, parrying Lithlannon's sword with his right-hand club. An instant later, however, he leaped toward the entrance to his lair, giving a grunt as if the movement pained him, then backing inside, two clubs at the ready. Just before he went out of sight, he shook off the cord from around his wrist, and Krinneth saw the cord was attached to a pair of short, heavy darts, one at each end.

He turned to the Facherlein. They were standing around what looked like a short but powerful crossbow mounted on a tripod. He picked up the cord and the darts, and went over to inspect Vohalton.

The Elf was only a little winded and had a tender spot in the middle of his chest. "When we stop tonight, I will put some salve on it," said Lithlannon.

"Good," grumbled Vohalton. "It feels as though my ribs have been crushed to powder. I would say I am lucky it was only a glancing blow."

"Yes. A wound from one of those spikes would have been much more serious." She looked around. "Where did that cord come from, the one that wrapped around the monster's arm?"

"Ah, that was ours." Landi was now standing behind them. "It is a weapon of our own devising, though we had not hoped to prove it on this journey. You see, there are two darts attached to the cord." He took the apparatus from Krinneth's hand and indicated the various things with a short, thick finger.

"The arrows are balanced and fletched so as to fly off to the side, one to the right and one to the left, pulling the cord between them. The cord strikes whatever is to be entangled, and the force of the arrows wrap it round and round. If it were to take a man at shoulder height, for instance, it would tie him up completely, allowing time to either escape from him or to take him prisoner."

"Good, good, very, very good," interrupted Michmesh, wings abuzz with urgency. "And we have been making enough noise to be heard from the other side of the city. Let us be packing up and moving quickly, before anything else is coming to see what is causing the disturbance. Quickly, quickly!"

A very little later, they had everything packed up and were moving on.

Chapter Twelve
THE OGRES' LAIR

The ogre's lair appeared to be a building, one which had lost its roof and some parts of its walls many years ago. In the fashion of ogres, the lack of a roof had been remedied, by some rough-and-ready method of putting in a few wooden pillars, running wooden rafters across from the walls, and piling brush, straw, and sod on top until it kept out the worst of the rain or melting snow. The walls had been patched by heaving chunks of masonry, poles, and a good bit of dirt up into the gaps, then encouraging willows and briars to take root.

There was no door, only a doorway, and out of that the ogres would eventually come for their nightly forays. Michmesh had found the party a place to camp and a place from which to watch the doorway. When the ogres had gone out, then they would go in and search for the Shield. At present, it was the turn of Krinneth to watch the doorway.

This kind of task gave him a great deal of leisure, perhaps too much leisure, for thinking. He was thinking about what he had said about the Puchlein and his poisoned arrows, how he was constantly learning more about his new surroundings. Would he ever come to feel at home here? Would he not always be expecting something new to happen, something which would cause him to realize how little he knew? Only in battle, only when he was striving with weapons, could he feel at all competent? And he knew he could not spend his whole nine years in battle or preparing for battle. What then? And what when his nine years were up? He had a place with Dhahal. That the king had promised. But what sort of place? And what would be his status? What could be the status of a man who had spent nine years in Faerie? Would anything but bad luck come of associating with such?

There was a possibility that Gwathlinn would wait for him, but that was not at all likely. Nine years was a long while, and in nine years, much would change. Dhahal might die, and in that case, what sort of place would Krinneth have? Would Dhahal's heir feel bound to hold by a promise he himself had not made?

He shook his head. If he had been a sentry, half an army could have walked into the camp while he was staring down at the ogre hole and thinking such grim thoughts! As it was, two or three ogres might have gone out or come in without him noticing. He was fairly sure that he had his eye on the hole all the time, though, and that his mind would have marked the passing of the monsters, however deep in thought he was.

There was a movement down there now; something was coming out of the entrance! He watched carefully. Yes, it was an ogre. The ogre was about as tall as the Dwaghebel, but heavier built. This one wore some sort of helmet on his head, a cap of roughly hammered iron. In one hand he held a long spear with a huge iron head, the other hand dangled empty at his hip.

The beast peered around carefully, examining the surrounding area. Krinneth remained very still; to move now would be to draw attention to himself. Now the ogre turned back to the hole; was he going back in? No, he moved further away, and four more ogres came out. He had probably come out first to see that all was safe.

The other ogres were like the first, save that none of them wore a helmet. One had a floppy leather cap, the others were bare-headed, showing a mat of wild black hair. They were all dressed in various sorts of skin clothing, jackets and trousers or kilts, with some sort of rough-and-ready shoes on their feet.

Two of the four bore spears much like that of the first, while the other two had short but heavy swords sheathed at their waists. The first ogre, apparently the leader, made a signal with his spear and set out walking. The other four followed behind him in single file.

Krinneth waited until they were out of sight, then slipped out of his hiding place and hurried to the camp. All the others looked up as he came in, expecting the news. "Five ogres have just left the lair."

"Five?" inquired Michmesh.

"Five." confirmed Krinneth.

"Good. We had been counting five of them, so all must be gone." Said Lithlannon.

"And they will not be back before morning?" asked Vohalton.

"Not very likely. In any case, we will be going in, finding the Shield, and coming out again. We ought to be being long-gone before they are returning, for certain, for certain."

"Let us go, then."

They moved rapidly through the ruins to the mouth of the ogres' lair, then slipped inside. Since most ogres know nothing of locks, the door was held shut only by a small boulder rolled in front of it. They easily dealt with this, then Lithlannon assigned Vohalton to stay and watch the door just in case.

The smell of ogre was strong at the door and grew more intense as they went further in. The building had originally had several rooms, but some of them were filled with rubble before the ogres had moved in. When they had come, they had sealed off some rooms altogether, and built others by the means of rough partitions in existing rooms. Had the party been required to conduct their own search for the treasure-rooms, they would most certainly have been a long time at it. Fortunately, Michmesh knew the way quite well, and led them unerringly.

After they had gotten some distance inside, Lithlannon had to call a halt while they lighted torches. Michmesh, whose eyesight was quite equal to the dimness of the ogres' lair, waited impatiently while they did so. When they were at last able to see their way properly again, they continued. Ogres were not notable housekeepers, and the bits and pieces of this and that which were revealed to the travellers' eyes caused Krinneth to think that the torches' light was a mixed blessing.

Michmesh flitted into a chamber, then flitted out again. Consternation was written on his face. "Things have been changing," he declared. "This is the room where the Shield was being kept, but it seems it is no longer being there."

The rest of the party went into the room and investigated.

There were a couple of rotting, broken chests whose contents, gold coins and jewellery, had spilled out across the floor. There were a few skin bags, also broken and losing their contents, and other than that, there was nothing. "When last we were being here," said Michmesh, "There was being much else in here. Many things are being gone, the shield among them."

"Moved perhaps to another room?" asked Lithlannon.

"Perhaps. It is hard to be being certain with ogres."

"Then we had better look around a little."

Michmesh sighed. "Yes, I suppose so. We will be having a little time before the ogres are returning. But let us not be taking the whole night."

"No. Michmesh, will you go back to warn Vohalton, tell him what has happened, and that we will be taking a little longer than we had first thought? I would not want him to be worrying about us. Then you can come back and guide us."

While the Puchlein was gone, they did a little looking around on their own. They found other rooms used to store treasure, but none contained the Shield. They found sleeping rooms of the ogres, where they did not linger because of the smell, and they found other rooms whose purposes were not quite clear.

When Michmesh rejoined them, they continued their search. With the number of rooms to look through, it took them some time, and towards the end, Michmesh was becoming nervous. Finally, he said, "I think we had better not be remaining here much longer. Some or all of the ogres will soon be returning, and if they find us here, we will be having trouble."

Lithlannon nodded. "Very well. We will look just a while longer, then we will go."

They went along, peering into each room in turn. The Puchlein hurried by one room without stopping, and Lithlannon called to him, "What of this room?"

"Only slaves and cattle will be living there. No need to bother."

"If there are slaves there, perhaps they will be able to tell us something." Lithlannon stepped inside the room, with Krinneth close behind.

Over in one corner was a small huddled group of sheep and goats, and in another corner was a group of goblins shackled together. They looked up dull-eyed as the searchers came in. Michmesh came up beside Lithlannon. "You will not be wanting to let these know just what it is that we are seeking, will you?"

She considered for a moment, then spoke. "No, but perhaps we can find out what we need without the necessity of being too specific." She walked closer to the goblins.

"Who of you would like to earn your freedom?"

For a moment there was no answer, then there was a small stirring in some of the dull eyes, a sort of goblin cunning reasserting itself.

"What sort of freedom?" asked one of them.

"We will be willing to break your chains and let you go if you can tell us what we wish to know."

"Break our chains and slay us, more like! We know you Elf-folk."

"No, I promise we will slay none of you, save that we will defend ourselves if attacked. By the Great Tree, I swear it."

"So, then. Tell us what you would know, and we will tell you if we know it."

"Have the ogres moved their treasure, and where have they moved it to?"

The goblins looked at each other in confusion. "Treasure? Moved?"

Then the one who had been the spokesman said, "They might well have moved it, and not have told us at all. For moving treasure, they would not likely trust us, slaves though we are."

"So you know nothing of where any of their treasure has gone?"

"No, only that two weeks ago they were forced to send a portion of it to Hoodaldow, the Ogre Lord. Oh, there was a real upset about that, I can tell you! An army of about fifty of them came to the door of this fellow here, Graychtblar the Furious he calls himself, and tells him that the Lord Hoodaldow demands a portion of his treasure. One part in one hundred, he said. Graychtblar and his fellows near exploded at that, and I thought there might be a fight, but five against fifty is bad odds, and even an ogre realizes that.

"They did what they could to hide part of their treasure, but the leader of the army was no fool either, and he took away a large part of it for all the blustering and threatening that Graychtblar could do."

Lithlannon nodded. "So. Krinneth, will you see to setting them free? And for those of you goblins who think you might attack us immediately upon being freed, look carefully; there is a Puchlein with an arrow on his bow, who does not trust you at all. And I, too, will have an arrow on my bow, and I can promise that the first of you who tries to attack will die."

The goblins stood patiently while Krinneth pried their manacles open, then one at a time, they went scurrying out the door and down the hallway. They could be heard stopping here and there to do some plundering, but the only thing they sought was the quickest way out.

When all the goblins were free, Krinneth went back to Lithlannon. "What do we do, then? Seek the hall of Hoodaldow the Ogre Lord?"

She shook her head. "I think not. Hoodaldow's Hall will be much better guarded than this, and less easy to approach. I think we will go back to Quarannon with what we have learned and let him make the decision."

Suddenly, Vohalton was at the door of the room. "The ogres have returned, Lithlannon! I am sorry, one would hardly expect something so large to move so softly, but they were on the doorstep before I was aware of them."

Lithlannon looked at Michmesh. "Michmesh, surely there is a rear way out of here."

He shrugged. "At least two that I know of, for certain, for certain."

"Then lead us to the nearest one."

They set out quickly, but the ogres had apparently noticed something amiss, perhaps a scent, perhaps the disorder of the lair was not disorder to the eyes of an ogre, and it had clearly been disturbed. "They are pursuing us, Lithlannon," said Michmesh.

"You can tell? All I hear is the shouting of ogres."

"Ah, but there may be shouting and shouting. This may be only the shouting of ogres pursuing intruders through their lair."

"Let us only stay ahead of them, then. Where are the Facherlein?"

Krinneth looked around. The three were nowhere in sight. "Where can they have gotten to?" He repeated Lithlannon's question.

She frowned. "They were warned; we cannot wait for them. I hate the thought, but we must leave them to fend for themselves." The shouts of the ogres took on a new note, and there was also the sound of heavy bodies falling. "They seem to be falling over things," panted Krinneth as they hurried along.

"If they can manage to break their necks, it will be as well with me," answered Vohalton.

Then the party were into a long straight hallway. "The door at the end is leading out," said Michmesh.

Footsteps sounded behind them, and Krinneth looked back. Landi, Gormi, and Varni were hurrying up behind them. Krinneth wondered where they had been, but he had no breath to ask questions.

This door, like the front door, was not a proper door, only a large slab of stone propped across the entranceway. They stared at it in dismay. Michmesh turned in chagrin. "I had been forgetting, you are not so small as we. We were going through that hole there, you see?" He pointed at a small gap in the lower left corner, where the stone did not quite cover the opening.

"Well, we have little choice. Let us see if we can push it."

They moved up to the stone slab and put backs and shoulders to it. Lithlannon announced, "One, two, three, push!"

They all heaved; the stone seemed to give a little, but then no more. Once again Lithlannon ordered, "One, two, three, push!"

The stone seemed to move a little more, then stuck. They could hear more roaring of the ogres behind them, but they dared not give any attention to that. Again they heaved, but this time the stone did not move at all. They tried once more, but there was still no movement. Panting, they looked around. "Well, only one of them can come at us at a time up this hallway. That is one advantage we have," said Vohalton.

"And even one at a time, five of them are likely to be too much for us. Stand away from the stone," commanded Lithlannon.

They stood back and watched. There was little to be seen, for she stood staring at the stone, eyes fixed to it, her face white with strain. She seemed to be humming, though there might have been words muttered in there, words in a strange rhythm which rose and fell and rose and fell again. Suddenly, the muttering broke off. She spoke a single loud word. At the same time, she slapped the rock with the flat of her right palm. There was a loud sound of breaking stone, and the large slab burst into fragments as though a gigantic hammer had hit it just where Lithlannon's hand had struck.

Lithlannon swayed a bit, and Krinneth and Vohalton took one arm each and rushed her out into the open air. The doorway had been camouflaged into a grassy hillside and as they came out, an ogre came rushing round the hill toward them.

Chapter Thirteen
THE WAY HOME

It was impossible to say whether the ogre happened to be coming by this way incidentally, or whether his chief had sent him to cut off the escape of the invaders. But either way, he was there in front of them, and had to be dealt with. Krinneth and Vohalton gently set Lithlannon down, then moved forward and to the sides, readying their weapons.

The ogre bore a short, broad-bladed sword, and grinned as he saw them. He said something in his own language, something Krinneth could not understand, but he was sure that it was no sort of friendly greeting. As the ogre sprang forward, raising his sword, Krinneth struck with Grothrion. It was only a glancing blow on the abdomen, but it staggered the ogre, and caused him to miss his own stroke. Krinneth, feeling the wind of that blow, knew that if the strike had landed, it would likely have been the death of him.

Vohalton sprang forward, drawing the monster's attention, and Krinneth struck one more blow. This time Grothrion hit squarely, and the ogre went down. Before he could rise, Krinneth struck once more, and that was that. At least, that was that, insofar as this one ogre was concerned. Three others were storming up along the long passage leading toward the back door. The Facherlein had set up their crossbow to aim into that passage, and just as Krinneth looked, they squeezed the trigger.

Unfortunately, just a little ways ahead of them, a small dead poplar protruded from the ground. One of the arrows bearing the cord struck that tree and stuck fast. The other continued on its way and, reaching the extent of the cord, swung around in a wide circle. The gnomes squawked and flung themselves to the ground as the arrow whipped by just over their heads.

It was not a complete failure, however. On its next circle, the arrow went around the knees of the foremost ogre, bringing him to the ground with an impact that was felt by all.

When he fell, he blocked the hallway sufficiently that the ogres behind him had to pause before they could get past him, giving Krinneth and his companions a little time to prepare. Lithlannon was on her feet now, obviously deathly weary, but just as clearly determined to do her part in this battle. She drew her bow and launched an arrow at the first ogre to approach. The arrow caught him full in the chest, causing him to stumble.

As Vohalton had taken advantage of the stumble of the first one, so Krinneth leaped forward with Grothrion swinging. It was still quite a battle; the ogres came up roaring, wielding their heavy weapons, and Krinneth and Vohalton dodged in and out to strike where they were able. Lithlannon hung back behind, loosing arrows as she found targets, and Michmesh, hovering at about the height of a man's shoulders, now and again sought a mark for his own envenomed little shafts.

Suddenly, the fight was over. Two of the ogres were dead, and the third was racing back along the passage, roaring with anger, fear, and the pain of several wounds. Michmesh looked around. "Quickly, quickly, let us be going quickly! With all that noise, there will be other things out and about for certain, for certain!"

Krinneth looked at Lithlannon. She smiled slightly, but her pale face betrayed her weariness. "Let us go. If Michmesh says that it is dangerous, it is dangerous. I will try not to hold you back."

They set off at a quick pace. The Facherlein, who had fought as well as they were able in the battle, looked longingly at their crossbow, but there was no time to disassemble it.

The Puchlein led them as one very familiar with the local trails, led them along the best paths which could be found. Krinneth was not sure why he felt that way, but there was something about the city now. That it was awake, watching and listening. Far off in the distance he heard sounds, the calls as of hunting beasts, but what beasts he could not tell.

Suddenly, ahead of them was a golden figure, the figure of a fair woman, who smiled and beckoned at them. "Be not looking!" called Michmesh. "As you are valuing your lives, be not looking in her eyes!"

They rushed on, and Krinneth, glancing out of the corner of his eye, saw that the colour was not gold, but a rather sickly yellow. And as the small party rushed on, he risked a glance at her face and saw it twist with rage.

On they went. From deep within a dark cavern came the sound of singing, such a fair and haunting song that they paused for a moment to hear it. Michmesh turned a frantic expression on them. "Be not stopping, be not listening! Do you be thinking that there could be anything in this city that would be meaning us anything but ill? Be moving, all!"

And on they went, though the song swept around them, calling to them, slowing their feet. Krinneth found himself repeatedly on the point of pausing only for a moment. Only a moment to hear the song, then he would go on. But each time he remembered Michmesh's warning, and each time he forced himself to continue.

From behind and around them, came a curious yipping bark. As they hurried along, Krinneth wondered what it could be, though thinking about Michmesh's injunction, he was sure it was nothing he would want to meet.

The Facherlein, loaded down with their packs, were stumping stolidly along, moving as though they could keep up the pace for days, if necessary. However, for Vohalton, the bruise on his chest hindering his breathing and was having a hard time of it, and Lithlannon was also obviously exhausted. Whoever or whatever was following them, the party would not be able to flee for very much longer.

The yipping bark was close behind them now. Krinneth put an arrow to his bow; from the sound of it, the pursuer was coming up rapidly. He turned to see the hound come around the bend in the trail. He had expected, from the bark, to see something small, but this was a hound nearly as high as his waist, a hound with a long squarish head and a mouthful of vicious teeth, and a pair of eyes which flickered with the light of hell.

He brought up his bow and loosed his arrow in a single motion, and was pleased to see the arrow take the hound directly in the chest. The beast ran on a few more steps, then fell, rolling forward with its momentum, and did not rise again.

Others were close behind him, and Krinneth took an arrow and picked another target. He loosed, and at almost the same moment one of the little shafts of the Puchlein arrows hissed over his shoulder. Two more hounds went down, but there were enough and to spare following along. There was no time for another arrow; Krinneth pulled Grothrion free from his belt and swung it.

There was another short melee then, and a few minutes of barking and snarling, red eyes and white teeth, swinging weapons and shouts of anger and fear. But the dogs did not flee; they attacked and fought. Krinneth swung Grothrion at the hounds and quickly noticed that they did not cower the way that the goblins had. However, when he hit them, they still took the same kind of damage. Hungry teeth snapped at him and Krinneth dodged out of the way. He wheeled around and swung at one of the hounds and connected. As he dispatched the hellhound the Puchlein's took down another, while Vohalton parried and thrust his own sword deep into another hound's belly. The companions looked around for any others before Michmesh called them to attention and led them off again.

Krinneth slipped one of Lithlannon's arms over his shoulders, and Vohalton did the same on the other side. She walked as best she could, but it was plain to see that she could not go much further.

The city which had seemed dead before was now alive with noise, the sounds of strange and fearful things on the hunting trail.

On they went, staying just ahead of the hunters. The trail wound and twisted, and sometimes Krinneth could tell that they were going down the remains of a broad street, sometimes they seemed to be picking their way through the fallen ruins of a large building. Still, other times there seemed to be no way to tell what this place was that they were hurrying through.

Lithlannon was hardly even keeping up a pretence of walking any more; though her feet kept moving, there seemed to be little strength in her legs. Vohalton was breathing in wheezy gasps on the other side of her, and Krinneth was sure they were altogether near the end of their strength. It wasn't long before they found themselves struggling up a lengthy but gentle slope. It was covered with thorns and willows, but under all this, Krinneth was able to distinguish the squarish shapes of huge hewn stones overgrown with moss and vegetation. This appeared to be the remains of the city wall. His spirits lifted for a moment, then he wondered if the things that pursued them would halt merely because they had reached the boundary of the old city. He struggled on.

The Facherlein had stopped and were doing something with some saplings, bending them over and tying them down. Snares? Here? What earthly good could they do? But he could spare neither breath nor energy to speak to them now; they knew as well as any the danger they were in, and if they chose to hazard themselves by stopping to do some typical piece of gnomish foolishness, he could not prevent them.

The slope fell off rather abruptly on the other side, so much so that the three, Krinneth, Lithlannon, and Vohalton, nearly tumbled head over heels. Krinneth caught himself and provided a steady balancing point for Vohalton. Lithlannon's head slumped on her chest, and her eyes were closed.

"A little further, a little further, only a few steps indeed, indeed!" called Michmesh. They forced themselves to carry on.

Before the party knew it, the Facherlein were hurrying along in their usual place; apparently, they had abandoned whatever they had been trying to do on the slope of the ruined wall. The party was in the forest now, amid the immense trees, still hastening along. Krinneth knew he would be unable to go much further, particularly not with him carrying half of Lithlannon's weight. He knew as well that Vohalton was in even worse condition, but Michmesh showed no sign of halting yet.

Then there was a new sound behind them, something that Krinneth could not quite make out, but the Facherlein cast glances over their shoulders, and their expressions seemed to be triumphant.

Michmesh led them off the trail, down through a shallow brook, into the midst of some overhanging willows. He smiled at them. "We will be resting here."

Krinneth and Vohalton set Lithlannon down as carefully as possible, then Vohalton himself slumped to the ground. Still gasping with the exertion he had gone through, Krinneth tried to keep some sort of watch on the back trail. He fixed his gaze down at the three gnomes. "Well, what did you do?"

Landi's eyes widened as he stared back up at him. "Which time?"

"Which time? You mean to say that there was more than once?"

"In the ogres' lair, as we came through, we set ropes tied to pegs across the hallway at about the height of an ogre's ankle. It slowed them, though perhaps not quite enough. On the wall, we set up some traps, jars of a very smelly liquid on bent trees; when the traps were set off, the jars flew in the air, spreading the liquid all over. For beasts who rely on their noses, it would make things difficult."

Krinneth smiled. "I had been thinking hard thoughts about you there on the ruined wall. I withdraw all those things."

The little man smiled slightly. "We try to please," he said.

Chapter Fourteen
IN ARLITH-YSTERVEN

King Quarannon heard the news gravely, propping his chin on one hand, and his elbow on the arm of his chair. "So the Shield was no longer there?"

"No, Lord King, it was not. I think the Shield was part of the treasure taken to Hoodaldow, as the goblins suggested."

They had taken their time coming back, after leaving Mathlabbin, and Lithlannon had an opportunity to rest herself. She now looked fit and healthy as ever, though Krinneth had been quite concerned about her while they remained in hiding in the willows.

"So. And I doubt it would be possible to take the Shield from Hoodaldow."

Lithlannon shook her head. "We have no way of knowing where in his house he has stored it. For that matter, he may have decided the Shield would make a suitable present to help ensure the continuing loyalty of one of his captains. Michmesh has agreed to pass the word among his folk, to see if they can track it down. I understand they can even creep into Hoodaldow's hold, at times.

"I know that there was little else to be done," said the King of the Elves, "but I could almost wish you had not spoken to the goblins, or set them free."

"But they do not know what we were seeking."

"No, but they do know that Elves are not given to idle hunts for treasure, particularly in the ruins of Mathlabbin. Now if one of them finds the King of the goblins and seeks to gain a little stature, might he not tell this news, that the Elves were seeking for something in the ruins of Mathlabbin, something which they knew to have been in an ogre's lair, and which was no longer there? And the conclusion must be that it had been taken to the Ogre Lord.

"And while Shtavrak and Hoodaldow are not on the best of terms, they are both allied against us, and might not Shtavrak send a messenger to suggest that Shtavrak look closely at the treasure he gained from Mathlabbin?"

"It would require several unlucky chances, and even then, would either Shtavrak or Hoodaldow know the Shield for what it was, even if they saw it?"

The King smiled. "Requiring even more unlucky chances, I know. And yet, we dare not entirely dismiss the possibility of such chances."

Lithlannon was quiet, considering all this. Krinneth spoke.

"I am speaking in ignorance, Lord King, but I do not understand why it is so vital that this shield be found. Is it not merely another old relic of bygone days?"

The King looked troubled. Even Lithlannon had an expression of concern. "The difficulty is," said the King, "that we do not know. The old tales tell us that Dys-Hanglorilar always bore the Shield Set with Onyx. Unlike the flail Grothrion however, there are no tales of great power regarding the Shield.

"Rather, it has no history at all before the time it came into the possession of the hero Dys-Hanglorilar. Yet in the years following the death of the hero, there have been prophecies which seem to hint that the Shield is important to the Elven Folk, and that it may have some strange power. But we do not know for certain."

He paused for a while, thinking, then he spoke once more. "There are small bits of lore, half-prophecies, which seem to tell us that the Shield is important. For instance:

The Shield was taken out to war,
And up into the hills it went.
The Shield it came back no more,

And woe to the Elven folk!
The Shield had never seen defeat,
And it marched to unequal strife.
And it was spurned by goblin feet,
And woe to the Elven folk!"

He looked up and smiled. "And what does all this mean? Only because we know of Dys-Hanglorilar do we connect this with him. And is the prophecy as serious as it sounds? Or does it merely mean that we have lost a hero who was sadly missed?

"Whichever it is, there are those among us who feel it would be foolish to ignore the situation. And on the other hand, whatever we do to search for the Shield must be done with circumspection; if our enemies get wind of what we are doing, they will probably begin their own search, if only to deny the Shield to us."

Then he smiled again, a bit ruefully. "However it is, we have no idea where the Shield has gone, and there is little to be done in that regard until we have a trail of some sort to follow."

For some days, then, Krinneth rested in the city of Arlith-ysterven. During the day, he practiced weapon-skill with Elven warriors, and studied the intricacies of the Elven language. In order to do so, he studied many old scrolls of Elven lore, and was occasionally amazed at his own ability for learning. In his old life, before he had come to Faerie, reading and writing were not skills common to a warrior. Here, however, it seemed it was an uncommon warrior who could not handle a pen as well as a sword or read a book as well as read an opponent's moves on the practice-field.

Lithlannon seemed intrigued by his newfound interest in learning. She would occasionally come by the book-house to find him busily reading. All too often, the first hint he would have of her presence was when he could feel eyes on him. He would look up from his books to find her there, dark eyes twinkling as she laughed. And so it happened again this time.

"So, at last you notice me! Now, had I been an enemy, you would certainly be dead!"

"If my enemies come seeking me in the book-house of Arlith-ysterven, then I think we are all doomed!"

"For certain, for certain, as Michmesh might say." Then she grew serious. "You are changing, Krinneth."

"I? Changing?"

"Yes indeed. You are no longer the warrior who first came into Faerie."

He considered that. "Yes, I suppose I have changed. But I think it was necessary if I were to live with the Elven folk for any time. You yourself act and think as much like an Elf as anything, for all the fact of your non-Elven heritage."

"Ah, but for me it came more natural; I came here as a babe, with no memory of anything else. I was brought up as an Elf and have lived my whole life as an Elf. You have come in as a grown man, and are consciously making yourself act like an Elf."

"And is that so bad? I shall have to live with these people for the next few years; is it not better that I should be as much like them as possible? Or ought I to be constantly throwing it into their faces that I am a man, and that I am different? I had to learn the language, at the very least. Once I began that, all the rest seems to follow naturally."

She was quiet, frowning to herself. After a silence, long enough that he was about to say something, anything, just to break it, she spoke. "Still, you are changing. And the change, however you see it, is a rather large one. When you go back, will you be able to leave this change behind?"

It was his turn to be silent, then. When he thought of it, he could see that she was right, that he was throwing himself whole-heartedly into life as an Elven warrior. Yet he still felt as he had, that it would be the worse for everyone if he did not at least try to adjust to his situation.

Then again, he could see that she was right. If he went back out of Faerie tomorrow, back to serve with Dhahal, would he miss all this?

He saw she was waiting for an answer, just as he had a few moments ago. He mustered his thoughts. "I suppose that all the change could not be left behind. Even so, I should have to do just as I am now, and make adjustments to my way of living so as to exist in the world outside." And yet, inside him, some small part of him cried out against such a return to that old life with all its restrictions.

The days passed by in Arlith-ysterven, and Krinneth found himself wondering what his next task would be. There had been no rumours or even hints, and even the goblins seemed to have settled down. There were occasional raids, none very serious, and most of them beaten off easily.

Though news from the goblin kingdom was not easy to come by, some news did come out. It appeared that Shtavrak was determined on war with the Elves, but there was some dissension in his kingdom regarding this and other matters. It would be some time, perhaps a year or more, before he could effectively make war against the Elves.

Quarannon had a short council regarding all this news. There were several factions, one of which wished to take this as good news and allow all their soldiers to go home. A smaller faction felt that this news, coming from goblins, could not be trusted, and was probably part of a goblin plan to make the Elves relax their guard, after which they would make a surprise attack.

Holvannon was one of the main spokesmen for this faction. "As long as we have known them, the goblins have been untrustworthy, making and breaking treaties as it suited them! Certainly this is good news we hear, but from whom do we hear it? From the small folk of the forest, who hear it secondhand themselves, from often doubtful sources! And we should believe this, and send all our troops home, leaving ourselves defenceless?"

Another faction consisted mostly of Elves of the outlying villages and settlements, Elves who recognized the necessity of banding together for defence, but who grudged every moment of time away from their fields, gardens, or crafts. Their spokesman was as vocal as Holvannon.

"Shall we be left defenceless indeed? And when Holvannon makes mock of the small folk of the forest, denigrating their reputation as gatherers of news, he should first recall that we of the outlying villages are more familiar with those small folk than ever the people of the cities will be. And for certain, one does not take every word they utter as being the final and absolute truth. Yet if we hear the same news repeatedly, then we can usually depend upon it to be reasonably accurate.

"And if we have so many saying that there is little danger, then we can be sure there is little danger. And if there is little danger, then why should we be here playing at soldiers when we could be home at our work?"

Others spoke, agreeing sometimes with one party and sometimes with the other, sometimes not quite agreeing with either. After they had heard many, Quarannon stood. "It would seem to me that we have heard all the views of our situation, and it now remains to decide. There are truths on both sides of the question; Holvannon is right, for instance, in saying that we can trust the goblins to be at war with us, and if they are not in the field with armies, they are back in their halls and homes, making plans for the next war. It behooves us to be prepared.

"On the other hand, there are more things to do than make war and train to make war, as our spokesman from the outlying villages has pointed out. Farms and gardens wither for want of hands to tend them, and such is perhaps as great a danger as being unready for a goblin attack.

"Thus, I have come to a decision. We will allow many of our warriors leave to go home to tend to their work. This will be done in a fashion which will allow us to have an army of some size always on hand. Leaders and captains, you will arrange these matters, seeing always that you balance fairness to individuals with the safety of the realm. If necessary, you may consult with me. If there are any immediate questions, you may come and talk to me in my quarters."

With that, he dismissed them.

FOR SOME WEEKS, LITTLE more happened. The goblins would make small raids, usually easily beaten off, then they would seemingly rest for a while, after which they would make another raid or two. Krinneth made a trip to one of the villages, which was often a target for such raids and was indeed present during one such. The goblins came howling in out of the night, but the village gave the alarm early enough that the goblins could be driven off.

It was a fierce little affair, done mostly by the light of flickering torches, but at the end of it the goblins fell back, having lost several warriors and without gaining much, save for what little they could grab as they fled. The Elves had also lost a few of their own, but in all, the defence had been a success.

Several more weeks went by without incident, then suddenly one day Lithlannon appeared in the village. After most of the villagers greeted them, she found time to take Krinneth aside.

"Next week will be three years since you came to us. Will you be going out to visit your friends, as was agreed?"

Krinneth was taken by surprise, for he honestly had to admit that he had lost track of the time. Suddenly, he realized Lithlannon was still standing there, awaiting an answer. "Yes, I suppose I ought to go, oughtn't I?"

Chapter Fifteen
OUT OF FAERIE

Krinneth sat, somewhat uncomfortably, at the table of Dhahal, son of Dalvin. It was no sort of consolation that the others at the table were as uncomfortable as he.

From his experience after the healing, he had expected this sort of thing, the staring and the warding symbols from people, the coolness from Gwathlinn, even from Dhahal himself.

To give him his due, Dhahal had rapidly overcome his initial reserve, and had embraced Krinneth warmly, welcoming him back among them. "Ah, lad, it is good to have you back again! You are well?"

"I am quite well, my Lord, but I am not back to stay, merely visiting. I have three days with you, then I must return to Faerie. As they promised, every three years I am allowed to come back for three days."

Dhahal had frowned a little at that. "Ah, yes. I see."

They had ordered the feast for that evening, and Krinneth was to be the guest of honour. And yet, when they were all gathered at the table of Dhahal, everyone showed some reluctance to speak to him, as though uncertain what to say. Since he was the guest of honour, it was necessary that much of the conversation should include him. Since he had also been away for three years, much of the normal talk of local happenings would mean little to him without explanations of what had passed in his absence. Few could endure such a prolonged conversation with him.

He could see by the faces that some wanted to ask him about his adventures in Faerie, but feared to do so. He tried to open conversations, hoping that once someone had begun speaking, they would forget where he had been, and begin treating him as one of themselves again.

Several times people had made reference to "Lord Kaldan's threshing," as though it had become a common expression. He knew of Lord Kaldan, but he could not conceive how the expression had come about, nor what it meant. Finally, when one of the younger men mentioned it, Krinneth took it upon himself to ask, "Gwathmal, what does this mean, 'Lord Kaldan's threshing? It has been mentioned several times this evening, but I have never heard it."

There was dead silence. Gwathmal looked up at him, a little fearfully, then looked down at the table and muttered. Straining his ears, Krinneth caught a confused tale of how Lord Kaldan, wishing to hurry his threshing along, had brought in some donkeys to tread out the grain alongside of the oxen, then brought in a few goats and sheep as well, only to find that goats and sheep were much less willing to be led or driven regularly around the threshing floor, ending with a great confusion.

Gwathmal's voice faded away, and he stole a quick look up under his brows at Krinneth, clearly hoping that this answer would satisfy the strange guest out of the strange land. Krinneth, for his part, considered only for a moment asking more questions in order to force a conversation, but realized in that same moment that it would gain nothing but more embarrassment for Gwathmal. Clearly, whatever he might say, they knew he had been away in Faerie all this time, and like as not he would put a curse on anyone who displeased him, even a little.

Dhahal, who was neither blind nor deaf to what was happening at his table, attempted to take a hand. He drew a deep breath and asked, "What is it like there, in Faerie?"

There was another dead silence, while people waited to hear what response Krinneth might make. He tried first to explain to them how much like themselves the Elves were, in their desire to simply live their own lives without being disturbed. He saw quickly that this would not be accepted, that they all knew was what strange and chancy folk the Elves were. As far as they were concerned, all Krinneth was doing was convincing them that the Elves had bespelled him against telling what they were truly like.

He went on then to describe the city of Arlith-ysterven, and many of its wonders. This the people found easier to believe, for it was the kind of thing to be expected of Elven folk. He also told of the goblins and their war against the Elves, and this evoked some sympathy, for goblins had been known from time to time to raid into the land outside Faerie, and their reputation was dark indeed.

He spoke also of the gryphons and other strange beasts, beasts that he had seen for himself and beasts which he had only heard of. Here, too, the people were willing to believe whatever he said, and he had a feeling that he could have made up whatever stories he wished about the beasts of Faerie, and have been believed.

"And what is it that you do there?" inquired Dhahal. "Do you make war against those goblins?"

There was a mutter of sound from the audience; this was the sort of thing they would have asked, had they dared.

"For now, yes," answered Krinneth. "My duties in Faerie are to serve the King of the Elves, to fight against his enemies, and to protect his realm. At present, the goblins are the greatest danger, but there are also others, such as the ogres and the Dark Elves, who may threaten us from time to time."

Someone, emboldened by the conversation, called out, "What of the magic of Faerie? With what spells have they entrusted you?"

A collective gasp erupted from most of the audience; this question, while it was much on their minds, was one they felt perhaps a little too bold, and they had a little fear of what Krinneth's response would be.

But Krinneth only laughed. "I know no magic at all, nor do I wish to. I follow the trade of the warrior, and that is enough for me."

The conversation was a little more free after that, though there was still a considerable reluctance on the part of most people to speak to Krinneth.

On the following day, Krinneth and Dhahal went out hunting. They had some success, and by the end of the day, most of those present had nearly forgotten the fact the Krinneth had spent three years in Faerie. There was another dinner that evening, though a smaller one than the previous night's, and more convivial. Gwathlinn was not present this evening, and Dhahal told Krinneth that she was apparently ill, and was dining in her own chamber, alone.

The next morning, Krinneth prepared to take his leave. He was out in the stable saddling his horse when Dhahal came out. It suddenly occurred to Krinneth that at no time had there been any mention of the crossbowman he had slain at the mere three years back. Perhaps Gwathlinn had told no one else what she was doing, and when the man did not come back, she continued to say nothing, knowing that it could only make her appear in a poor light.

And Krinneth knew that he himself had no intention of mentioning the matter; his reception had been bad enough without letting everyone know that he had slain one of Dhahal's crossbowmen in order to protect the Witch of the Westermoor.

"You leave today, then?"

"Yes. For three days I am allowed to visit, then I must return."

"Aye." Dhahal stood silently watching him for a time, and when he spoke, it was with a curious diffidence. "Gwathlinn would have me ask you to stay."

Krinneth nodded. "We spoke of that three years ago, when first I left. Nothing has changed, Lord. And as you yourself said, if I were the sort to go back on my sworn word, you would not want me here."

"Just so. And that is why I do not ask it of you. Be well, lad."

As he rode away, Krinneth found himself thinking that it was just as well that Gwathlinn had not come down to see him off. That thought made him feel strangely uneasy.

Chapter Sixteen
IN FAERIE ONCE MORE

By the time he had returned to Faerie, the uneasiness had mostly passed. He had half-wondered whether someone might be waiting for him at the edge of Faerie, and was surprised to find himself disappointed when they were not. And when he realized within his own mind that he had been hoping Lithlannon would be there, he felt uneasy again. Nothing further had been said regarding himself and Gwathlinn, but while the arrangement had not been confirmed, neither had it been specifically cancelled.

He rode on his way to Arlith-ysterven, and his thoughts were grim.

Lithlannon came to meet him at the gate of the city. Smiling at him, she asked, "How went it, then?"

"It was difficult, at the first, and only became a little less so later on. They do not wholly trust me. I think it will take some time for them to become used to me again when I finally leave here."

She nodded. "People fear that which they do not know. It happens, even among the Elves; there are some here who mistrust you because you are human."

THE DAYS PASSED BY in Arlith-ysterven, and Krinneth spent his time training with the Elvish warriors. From time to time, he would visit the outlying villages, occasionally coming in time to fight off a goblin raid. Such raids had become fewer now, one a month or less.

With the lessening of the goblin raids, some of the vigilance of the Elves also slackened.

Though they had agreed that the outlying villages should constantly send youngsters in to be trained, and to serve in the army for a term of years, the young warriors no longer came in regularly. The King would send messages to the outlying villages reminding them of their obligations, and grudgingly warriors would come in.

After a time, the warriors were coming in only in response to the King's messages. Eventually, even the most severe reprimand would bring in only a few, much fewer than originally agreed on, and those warriors were usually not at all pleased to be sent on what was coming to be considered a time-wasting duty.

Holvannon was angry over the situation and made his feelings well-known in council. "They made promises and agreements, and see what those promises and agreements mean to them! It is time we ceased to allow such behaviour!"

"And how would you halt it, Holvannon?" asked the King.

"How? I would cease to send polite messages to them, begging them to send the people they had agreed to send! If the contingents are not here, in full strength, on the day when they are supposed to be here, then we send out a patrol to bring them in, whether or not they come willingly!"

"And do you think that will make them love us the more, there in the outlying villages?"

"Love us? What do we care if they love us, so long as they send in the troops we need?"

"Ah, yes," said the King, quietly. "The troops we need. And this is exactly their point; why do we need all these troops?"

"Why? My Lord King, we argued that out in council long time back. We need the troops to protect us, all of us, both we in Arlith-ysterven and the folk of the outlying villages!"

The King nodded. "Even so. You see this, I see this, but most of them see only that they have had relative peace for most of two years now, and if that is the case, why send more young Elves off to be soldiers when they could be more profitably employed at home? These are the sorts of messages I am constantly receiving, Holvannon."

"Then they think that we are safe because the goblins have left us alone for a little while? My Lord King, that is folly!" "I agree, yet what are we to do? If the goblins do not threaten us, the village folk will not believe we are under a threat."

"And they will believe there is a threat only after the goblins have come forth in such numbers that we cannot hold them back? My Lord King, you ask what we are to do; I tell you, we should send out armed bands to bring in the contingents, if we can get them no other way!"

"Indeed, Holvannon, we could begin to bring in contingents in such a manner. But if you have to bring in unwilling troops under guard, what sort of soldiers will they make? Would you trust your life to such? Would you be willing to depend on them to do more than desert and go back to their villages the moment your back was turned?"

"If we see to it that such desertion is punished—-"

"Holvannon, I beg your pardon, but I have considered all this and rejected it. We would then have a situation where the folk in the outlying villages hate and distrust us. They now send in contingents grudgingly; they would no longer send them in at all, except under force. Most of our trained troops would then have their time taken up by travelling from village to village, bringing in conscripts, and hunting down those who have deserted.

"No, I like this not at all, having to send messages continually in order to bring in a few youngsters to be trained, having to make do with what I know are too few. The alternative, however, is even worse.

"All I can do is to ask that you be careful and watchful. Whenever there is any sign that the goblins may come forth in strength, ensure that I know immediately. Such a threat may well encourage those who have been dilatory. And then we must hope that it will not be too late."

There was still nothing specific for Krinneth to do, so he filled his time with helping to train the contingents which came in, and with his various other studies.

The more experienced captains of the Elf-warriors took it in turns to command garrisons toward the outer part of the realm, and eventually Holvannon was sent out to one of the forts. Krinneth would willingly have taken on such a command, but none was offered to him. One day, while he was overseeing the arms-practice of a band of recruits, he looked up to see Quarannon standing off to one side, watching.

The King beckoned to him. Leaving the recruits to practice on their own, Krinneth walked over to where the King was standing. "You are no fool, Krinneth. You will have noticed already that while everyone else takes a turn at the command of one of the garrisons, we have not yet asked you to do so. Rather than let you wonder about this, and perhaps suspect us of evil intent, I thought it best to explain to you.

"You are being kept aside because Lithlannon has a feeling, something akin to a prophetic vision, save not so clear, that you have a particular role to play, and that role requires you to be free to act and to move as you must. Putting you into command of a garrison would prevent that, and thus, you are being kept aside."

The King paused, looked at the sweating recruits for a moment, then turned back to Krinneth. "Since you are no fool, as I have already said, you will already well know there are a good many Elves who would take it hard if I put you in command of them. But I wish you to know that it is not for fear of such that I keep you out of command." He looked at Krinneth with a smile. "Again, you have only my word for my reasons, but I assure you I tell the truth."

"My Lord King, you need not assure me of that."

FINALLY, ONE NIGHT, Quarannon summoned Krinneth. Krinneth could tell from the expression on the face of the Elf-King that there was trouble. "Holvannon sends word that the goblins have been trying the defences in his area. He would like to see us send him fifty to a hundred seasoned warriors, but such warriors are not easy to be found. All I can muster for him are twenty lads, all trained in arms, but none of them with any experience in battle. Will you take these reinforcements to Holvannon?"

"I am willing enough to do so, Lord King, but what will Holvannon say? He has little use for my kind, you know."

The King nodded. "Yes, I know. But he is a soldier like yourself, and he will follow orders. I am sending you with the youngsters because I hope that Grothrion will help to make up the lack of numbers. And Holvannon, if he is wise, will welcome the reinforcements, no matter the guise in which they come."

"As you command, Lord King."

Once again, the Facherlein were demonstrating their flying machine in the dining hall. This time, though, their audience consisted mostly of the elderly and the very young. Varti gave a brief speech beforehand. "Since the last time we demonstrated this machine to you, we have made some changes and modifications, particularly in the wing-structure. It is hoped that this time it will work properly."

They lit the fire-pot and stoked the flame carefully. As the assembled Elves watched, it smoked and steamed, then finally one of the gnomes stepped in to tap the mechanism. The huge wings began to beat, but this time there was something different to the way they were beating. They seemed to flex as they went upward and remaining stiff on the downbeat.

The wings beat quicker and quicker as the machine moved faster and faster. At first the machine showed no sign of flight, indeed no sign of any movement at all, then it gave tiny hops across the table. Before anyone was quite aware of what was happening, the machine had reached the edge of the table, and the next hop took it over.

The machine dropped like a stone, but at the last moment before it hit, it seemed almost on the point of lifting up. Then it crashed to the floor, and as Elves dodged back away from it, the great wings dashed themselves against the chairs and tables. Steam and smoke came from the mechanism, and one of the three gnomes dashed in with a bucket of water, throwing it over the whole thing. There was a cloud of steam, only partly dispelled by the last few movements of the wings, as they flapped slower and slower, then stopped altogether.

The Facherlein calmly gathered up the pieces of their machine, then Varti stepped forward. He seemed no whit more embarrassed this time than he had been at the previous failure of the flying machine. "I beg your pardon, Lords and ladies. We have apparently not quite yet perfected the technique. We shall have to make a few more adjustments to our machine."

Chapter Seventeen
THE FORTRESS HARGLYTH-NASHWER

The Fortress Harglyth-Nashwer, which translated as 'Golden-red Twilight,' was far from the center of the Elven lands. It was, in fact, on the very edge of the Elven lands, facing the land of the goblins. It had been established many years ago, during one of the earlier wars between the two peoples. Its function had been to house a garrison of troops to give warning of the approach of goblin armies, and to hold out until the armies of the Elves could come to relieve them.

Holvannon, who was commander of the garrison, watched with distaste as the reinforcements marched in. The warriors of his command, taking their cue from him, looked on, sneering.

Krinneth, after bringing his troops to a halt, marched over to Holvannon. "I bring you reinforcements, commander."

Holvannon looked from the new troops to Krinneth and back again. "Do you indeed? By the First Light, I ask for a force of warriors, and I am sent an outlander in charge of twenty children!"

He spoke loudly enough to be heard not only by those near to him, but by the newcomers as well.

Krinneth glanced at him but said nothing. Instead, he turned to his own troops and called them to attention. "I am sorry, but we appear to have come to a place where we are not wanted. Since the commander here does not feel the need of our services, we shall have to go back to the King and ask him to send us somewhere where we can be of use. And since we are not welcome here, we will have to go now."

He took his place at their head and led them to the gate. For a moment Holvannon stood dumbfounded, then he strode across to confront Krinneth at the gate. "What do you do, outlander?" he demanded.

"We were sent by the King to reinforce you. However, you have clearly shown that you do not want us here, so we are leaving."

"Leaving? Leaving? You will desert, then?"

"Not at all. We will go back to the King and tell him you apparently thought our help superfluous, and ask him to send us somewhere where we are needed."

"Needed? Outlander, I need every warrior I can muster, and probably more!"

"And if all the warriors that can be spared for you are twenty children and an outlander?"

To give him his due, Holvannon realized he was at fault and tried to make amends. His gaze did not fall on Krinneth, but on the troops Krinneth had brought in, as he spoke.

"I beg your pardon, Elves. I spoke in haste, and in disappointment, for I had requested a hundred warriors, fifty at the least, and they have sent me twenty. In the last weeks, we have been preparing for an attack by goblins, in which we fully expect to be outnumbered at least three to one. And since there are only twenty of you to take the place of the hundred I had asked for, you will each have to fight as five if we are to survive. Will you do that?"

Krinneth turned to the troops and said, "Well, lads, will you?"

They answered in a loud, affirmative shout. Lithlannon came strolling up from the end of the line. "Well done, Holvannon. I think you may have almost redeemed your first hasty words."

He looked at her, then looked again. "Lithlannon! What do you do here?"

She smiled. "What do I do here? Why, just what all the others do, I expect. I am here to help reinforce you."

"And the King allowed you to come?"

"The King? The King very seldom allows me or disallows me. Oftentimes he asks or requests, and most times I do what he asks or requests, but the choice is always mine. And this time I chose to come here."

"I do not like this at all, Lithlannon!"

"Why not? Have I not proved my worth from time to time upon the battlefield? Do you seek to insult me as well, Holvannon?"

Her smile took a little of the sting out of her words, but not much. Holvannon subsided with a mutter.

For the next few weeks, they worked themselves into the routine of garrison life. At first, the new troops who had been brought in by Krinneth were looked at contemptuously by the older and more experienced Elves of the garrison. This did not escape the notice of Holvannon, who recognized it as potential danger; if his troops were divided amongst themselves, they would be that much less effective in battle, were every one of them would depend on all the rest. He took the newcomers and divided them up among the existing companies, leaving it to the commanders of those companies to see that the fresh troops fitted in.

In a private talk, he confessed to not being sure what to do with Lithlannon or Krinneth. "Neither of you is an ordinary warrior, and if I were to put you into one of the companies, it might be taken as a hint by some that the commander of that company was failing, and that I was preparing the way for you to take his place. And I cannot put you into some sort of command, promoting you over the heads of those who have served here well and faithfully for many days. Do you have any suggestions?"

Krinneth pondered the matter. Finally, he spoke. "You are right. It will be difficult to fit us into the garrison as you have organized it. Best leave us out altogether; we will not command any troops, nor be under the command of anyone save yourself. We will carry out scouting duties, and various other such matters, so that none can say that we are shirking. And when it comes to fighting, you can send us anywhere. When another sword is vitally needed, few will ask questions about where it comes from, or why."

Holvannon smiled then, just a little. "And if it is the flail of Grothrion, they will even be grateful."

The day after that, the Facherlein came in. The sentry at the gate gave the alarm, mistaking the stumpy bodies weighted with packsacks and bundles for the squat and stumpy bodies of goblins. Elves scrambled from their barracks, seizing weapons from the racks as they rushed to the walls. When the storming party of goblins was only three, and those three not goblins at all, but gnomes, there was a good deal of muttering among those who had been interrupted in what they considered being more important pursuits.

Holvannon sought out Krinneth. "Were you expecting these?"

"No, I was not expecting them, but I am not surprised to see them here."

"So you can see to rations and quarters for them. And see to it they understand that this is not some quaint and amusing place to visit, but a fortress on the edge of enemy territory. If they are going to be here, they will have to do their share."

"I doubt that they had intended anything else," answered Krinneth. Then, as Holvannon walked away, he muttered, "At least, I sincerely hope that they intended nothing else."

Lithlannon appeared at his side, as if by magic. "Who intended nothing else?"

"The Little Folk, I hope." He looked up at her. "I was trying to mollify Holvannon; in point of fact, I doubt that the Facherlein considered any intentions beyond staying with the two of us. Have you ever discovered what it is about us that has attracted them?"

She shook her head, causing her dark hair to swing. "Too often when they begin to explain things, they do so in a manner which only makes things less clear. Ah well, let us go talk to them. Belike, we will be able to convince them to avoid irritating Holvannon."

But the Facherlein seemed to understand perfectly about the necessity of staying on good terms with Holvannon. Among other things, they immediately set up a sort of smithy and began to work at all the sorts of repairs which would be necessary in a warriors' camp, from sprung rivets in dagger hilts, to the actual production of new blades. They made themselves so useful that after they had been in Harglyth-Nashwer for two weeks, the entire garrison would have been sorry to see them go.

For a long time, matters were quiet around Harglyth-Nashwer. Some of the newcomers had wondered (though never out loud) if Holvannon's requests for more reinforcements had perhaps been based on a threat more perceived than real.

There came a day, however, when a messenger came staggering in through the gate with an arrow in his back. That arrow told the story, for there was not one among them, however new, who did not know goblin-fletching when he saw it.

The Elf was badly wounded, but he could tell where and how many, and with that knowledge, Holvannon sent out his second in command with a considerable portion of the garrison.

He talked with all his commanders before sending out the force. Because of their status, Lithlannon and Krinneth were also present. "It is quite possible that this whole raid was intended to lure us out from behind these walls, where their numbers will count for more. Our scouts say that there are no large numbers of goblins within ten miles of Harglyth-Nashwer, but that means only that they are at least ten miles away, and we all know how quickly an army of goblins can march.

"Therefore, I charge you, Dys-Lumill, be wary. If there seem to be more goblins than you expect, return here quickly. Whatever else we lose, we cannot afford to lose soldiers. Is this all clear?"

"All quite clear, Commander."

"Then go, and may good luck, go with you."

After Dys-Lumill led his force out, Holvannon became ever more concerned about scouting the neighbourhood of the fortress. Krinneth and Lithlannon, in their guise as special scouts, went out day after day. At first, there was never a sign of goblins in the area. Then they found traces of the passage of small parties of goblins, apparently scouting the area themselves.

This news caused Holvannon to become even more terse and short-tempered, and it was clear he was toying with the idea of sending out a messenger to call back Dys-Lumill and his detachment.

He held back, however, because there was always the possibility that this was merely some sort of feint by the goblins, intended for just such a result, to force the Elves to draw back to their fortress while the goblins plundered the villages.

At about the same time, messages came from the King of the Elves. These messages were brought by birds. Certain Elves had a gift of being able to talk to birds and animals, and even often to convince the bird or animal to do them a small service. Such gifts were valued, for though all Elves had closer ties with things of nature than other folk, rarely was the tie so strong.

Krinneth saw the birds arrive and guessed the import of the messages from the look on Holvannon's face afterward. Krinneth spoke to Lithlannon. "It appears that there are bad tidings."

"It would appear so. At a guess, I would say that the King is informing us that he can send no more reinforcements to us."

Krinneth chuckled. "That much would have been obvious to a blind man. I was wondering exactly what the news was."

"You might go ask." Her eyes were laughing.

"And I might hurl myself from the walls of the fortress. In either case, I would deserve what damage I suffered."

"Ah," she said, "I see where this is leading. You hope to convince me to go talk to him so that I can bring the news back to you."

"No, not necessarily. Holvannon is the kind of leader who lets his troops know what they are facing. Sometime soon he will gather us together and tell us essentially what the messages say. Though I am curious, and if you should happen to find out before he tells everyone, I would appreciate your letting me know."

She put her hands on her hips and looked at him in mock anger. "I thought as much! You do not care for me at all, only for what I might do for you!"

"But you do it so well!"

Even as he framed his mocking answer, Krinneth realized that in truth, he cared for Lithlannon. And the idea was something of a shock to him, for he was only to be here for nine years, and then he would leave, going back to Gwathlinn. Or would he? Would Gwathlinn wait another six years for him?

And that thought caused him to think of something else. Was he hoping that Gwathlinn would wait, or hoping that she would not?

Then he noticed Lithlannon was looking at him again, but the laughter was gone from her face, and there was deep concern instead. "What is it, Krinneth? Is something wrong?"

He forced himself to smile. "Other than the fact that we seem likely to be attacked by goblins in great numbers, we can expect no reinforcements, and our commander dislikes me, probably nothing."

She returned a smile, but he could tell she did not really believe him.

But as Krinneth had predicted, Holvannon called them all together later that afternoon to speak to them.

"If there is anyone here who has not heard of the messengers arriving this afternoon, I would be surprised. I would be even more surprised if there were not also at least three versions extant of the message they brought." He smiled wryly at them and went on. "For that reason, and in order that none of you should be deluded regarding our situation, I have called you together.

"The goblins are marching on Grysanth, Hladhlandon, Visitirrin, and Glys-Branthen. Whatever reinforcements the King can gather must be sent to those places, so we must hold with what we have here. In actual fact, the words of the King were that I should decide whether or not we can hold with what we have. If not, we should destroy this fortress and go back to Arlith-ysterven.

"I have decided that we can hold, and so we will. It is entirely possible that the goblins will attack in sufficient force to take this fortress, in which case we will all be dead, though some may live to be slaves of the goblins. If there are any of you who dislike either fate, let you step forward. You may go back to Arlith-ysterven, and there shall be no shame on you for it."

The entire group was suddenly extremely still. Krinneth, at the rear, smiled slightly to himself as he realized what was happening. No one wanted his neighbours to think he had even entertained the notion of leaving and, because the slightest movement might be misunderstood, they were all standing as still as possible.

Holvannon's cold, steely eyes slowly surveyed them all, giving the group a little time to think about his offer. No one moved. Finally, he nodded. "Good. I had thought none of you would wish to go. Indeed, we may not be attacked at all. However, in order to protect ourselves better, we shall do more scouting and patrolling. The goblins have been patrolling this neighbourhood themselves, and they rarely do that sort of thing merely for the look of it.

"So. Now you all know as much as I do. Back to your work, all of you."

Two days later, Krinneth and Lithlannon were out scouting, checking the area immediately around the fortress for signs of goblins. In this sort of activity Krinneth was quite used to following Lithlannon's lead, for he recognized that she was a natural leader and more experienced than he, indeed probably much better than he would ever be. For all their raillery and joshing in the fortress, while they were outside, they were quite serious.

He watched her suddenly press herself against an oak tree, making a small motion with her head. He read the motion to mean she heard or sensed something on the trail ahead. Both of them were in the habit of scouting with an arrow ready, so when the time came, they need not fear alerting an enemy by the sound of an arrow coming out of the quiver. She carefully set her arrow on the bowstring, and he followed suit.

He himself could hear nothing, but he was quite willing to trust her senses. If it were goblins, he wondered how many. The chances were that it would be only a group of scouts, anywhere from five to twenty. In the latter case, he and Lithlannon might have difficulty escaping, though they had an advantage in knowing these woods better than any goblins were likely to.

He peered carefully around the bole of the tree. A goblin was walking down the centre of the path, watching carefully from side to side. Like Krinneth and Lithlannon, he had a long black arrow on his thick recurved bow. Also, like Krinneth or Lithlannon, he wore dark leather; metal armour had a distressing tendency to jingle or clink at just the wrong moment.

The goblin looked directly at Lithlannon, but appeared not to see her; Elf or not, she had much of the Elven ability to remain unseen in wooded country. Krinneth knew that he himself had little, if any, such ability, but he might slip around the trunk of the tree and remain unseen. Unfortunately, the goblin had companions coming along the trail behind him, and one of them was likely to see Krinneth from the other side; the tree was not that thick.

He moved slowly and carefully up to where he would be almost visible to the others. Then he stood still and waited. The goblin moved along the trail, still sweeping his gaze from left to right and back again. Krinneth held his breath. The goblin stared right at him, then looked away again. For an instant Krinneth thought he had succeeded in remaining unseen, then the goblin's head was swinging back suddenly and he was bringing his bow up.

Krinneth needed less time to bring his bow into line, and he loosed his arrow before the goblin could even draw, and the goblin fell with a sort of strangled squawk.

Immediately upon seeing their comrade go down, the other goblins sprang off the trail. While not quite so proficient as Elves, goblins have a fair ability to hide among trees and rocks, and as soon as they left the trail, three of them were nigh unto invisible. His quick count told him there were probably not more than four more of them, but there might be more coming up.

He took quick aim at the one which he could see, loosed his arrow, then knelt quickly to be hid by the foliage.

There was another squawk; had he hit again? There was little to see as he peered out as best he could. He thought he saw a movement, then an arrow whipped through the foliage just above his head, cutting off a small twig. He set another arrow to the string, peering at the place where he thought to have seen the movement. Was there something there, or was it his imagination?

An arrow struck the oak well above his head, but he did not know where that one had come from. He heard the sound of a bow from up where Lithlannon was hiding, and another goblin yelped, stood, and fell face-down onto the ground.

This time he was certain he saw a movement; he drew his bow quickly and loosed, but there was no reaction. He brought out another arrow, then almost yelped himself as he felt a blow on his left forearm and a black arrow was suddenly there, driven through so hard that half its length stood out on the other side.

He had seen no movement that time, but he heard Lithlannon's bow again. There was the sound of movement across the trail, but it died away quickly, and he saw nothing. Another arrow whipped past his head; this time he was almost certain he saw a fierce yellow eye glaring at him, and he loosed an arrow. He heard it hit home, but there was no sign of the goblin. For a long time, there was no movement.

He waited, peering carefully out. From the way the goblins had been shooting at him, he knew he was not very well hidden. But he knew if he moved, he would very likely expose himself even worse. So he waited.

He heard a whistle from across the trail. Lithlannon called quietly, "Krinneth! I am coming out! Don't shoot!"

He stood up. "Come on, then."

And sure enough, there she came from across the trail. He had not even seen her go across.

"They are all dead, Krinneth." Suddenly she saw his arm, with the arrow still through it, and an expression of concern suddenly came over her. "You are wounded!"

"Not badly," he protested, but suddenly noticed a feeling of weakness. He had clearly lost a good deal of blood. He sat down suddenly.

Lithlannon quickly busied herself over his arm, snapping off the barbed head of the arrow so the shaft could be pulled out, during which time he clenched his teeth tightly so as not to cry out. She also sprinkled some special herbs on both wounds, then bound them up in clean cloth. Amidst all this, she gave him a water-bottle and bade him drink deeply.

When it was all done, she smiled at him. "It will heal, and probably quite quickly. The healing I performed on you back at the Westermoor its power still remains with you to some extent."

"Very good. But belike we ought to be moving along. There may be more goblins coming shortly."

"You think so?" But even as she spoke, she raised her head, listening. He could hear the silence as well, as though all the birds had ceased to sing, and all the beasts who roamed the forest had stopped still.

"They come already, and plainly over ten or twenty. We had best move immediately."

He got to his feet and noticed how shaky he still was. "You go on. I cannot move fast enough to stay ahead of them."

"Nonsense! I will not leave you behind. Come with me."

She moved not along the trail but further off it.

"They will look around when they find their dead scouts, and they will follow us."

"They will try to follow us. With a little care, we can lose them."

"And then what? This seems to be a large army, and they will very likely be besieging the fortress. We will be cut off."

"That may be as that may be. Better so than dead." She continued to walk through the woods.

Chapter Eighteen
THE BATTLE OF HARGLYTH-NASHWER

"I think we may have eluded them," said Lithlannon.

"I hope so. But they have proven themselves very determined pursuers before now."

They were crouched in the shelter of a stand of willows, which kept a little of the rain off them. They had been playing hide and seek with the goblins for three days now, during the first day of which Krinneth was somewhat weakened by his wound. During that time, the main body of the goblins had passed them by on the way to the fortress.

As Lithlannon had predicted, however, Krinneth healed quickly. Indeed, he was much better by the second day and by today, aside from an occasional ache in his arm, it was as though he had never been wounded.

She smiled. "Well, consider this, Krinneth. Goblins like wandering around forests in the pouring rain even less than you or I. It is very likely that those who have been ordered to search for us will have pitched their tents somewhere and will eventually go on back to their leaders to say that our trail has been washed away."

"If we have eluded them, then what ought we to do now? Try to slip through their lines back into the fortress?"

She frowned. "We might attempt that indeed, if it comes down to the end of our choices. I think rather that we ought to seek out Dys-Lumyll."

It was Krinneth's turn to frown. "Is Dys-Lumyll still alive? I suspect now that the whole point of all the raids was to convince Holvannon to send out a small force which could be ambushed and destroyed, thus weakening the garrison for this attack."

"Even so, we ought to go see for ourselves. Consider how hard the goblins are hunting us; would they seek so hard for two Elves? But if there were a possibility that those two Elves might come back along with others to attack the goblins from behind, then they might well be wary."

In most things, they discussed matters until they could come to a mutually satisfactory arrangement. There was an unspoken agreement, however, that Lithlannon was in command. And if, after all the discussion was over, she decided that a thing should be done, it would be done.

In time of combat, Lithlannon gave orders and Krinneth obeyed them. In fact, they worked so well together that Lithlannon rarely needed to give orders, for she usually found Krinneth doing already what she was about to command him to do.

"Do we go tonight, then?"

"No, we will try to get what rest we can and leave in the morning."

They set up a small shelter, enough to keep the rain out, then they had a meal consisting of a few sips of water and a few bites of bread. The bread was no ordinary bread, but a special sort baked by the Elves for war or travelling, so that a few bites were enough to sustain the body for a long while. However sustaining this Elven bread might be, it was not at all filling and its taste was only mediocre.

"Ah, it will be good to get somewhere where there is more to eat than this bread! I know it feeds me all I need, but could they not have improved the taste?"

Lithlannon smiled. "I have been led to understand, by certain wise people, that there is a reason even for the taste. The Elven bread could indeed have been made delicious, but what then? A fine taste might lead people to eat more than they needed, to devour several days' worth at one sitting. This way, it encourages us to make it last."

He looked at the bread. "It makes a certain kind of sense, I suppose. But I still wish for something large and solid, such as half a horse, or the like."

She grinned. "Your stomach will help you stay awake on watch tonight, to ensure that you live to eat your banquet."

In fact, neither one of them slept very well that night, what with hunger and the fact the rain did not stop all night long. In the morning, only a little rested, they set out.

During the first day and a half, the rain continued. Once or twice it let up almost to the point of stopping, but just when Krinneth was about to remark on it, the rain would begin pouring down harder than ever. Then, about noon of the second day, as suddenly as it had begun, the rain ended. Equally suddenly, the clouds broke up, and the sun shone brightly.

They marched steadily along the trail, somewhat cheered by the weather, and suddenly Lithlannon stopped. She stepped off the trail quickly and Krinneth, without a word, followed suit. "It was a bird-call," she said, "and so well done that it seemed almost to come from an actual bird. But it was a nesting-call, and at this time of the year, that bird would not likely make that call. I assume it is one of Dys-Lumyll's scouts, but it is best to be cautious."

They waited. A little later a voice called out, "Lithlannon! Is that you?"

"It is I." She stepped out into the trail, and another Elf stepped out to face her.

"What do you do so far from the fortress?"

"I think that is a tale we had best tell to Dys-Lumyll." The Elf's face went a little grave. "I regret, Lithlannon, that Dys-Lumyll was killed in a goblin ambush two days ago."

"Who is in command, then?"

"Well, Gladron, I suppose."

"You sound doubtful."

"Well, it is only that not everyone is willing to accept commands from Gladron. There are a few who feel very strongly that the goblins are too many in this part of the country, and that we would be best to go back to Arlith-ysterven as quickly as possible, in order to protect the city, at least."

"And how many are there altogether in the group?"

"Fifty-three, unless some of the objectors have already slipped away to return to the city."

Lithlannon frowned. "It is that bad? We had better talk with your people."

There were still fifty-three Elves with Gladron, though when they gathered together to hear what Lithlannon had to say, it was obvious there were several them who were on the point of desertion. They stood around the outer edge of the group, leaning on spears, watching with frankly hostile eyes.

Lithlannon spoke first to Gladron, in quiet tones. "What happened?"

The other shrugged. "We wandered here and there, looking for goblins. It almost seemed that they knew where we were going and when we would arrive. Then we came upon the track of the entire army, which was attempting to bypass us and make for Harglyth-Nashwer.

"We raced to get ahead of them, but again, it appeared they were aware of our intentions before we had formed them. Along our path, they set up an ambush. And we, with all our minds concentrated on rushing along to reach the fortress, rushed right into the ambush.

"Dys-Lumyll, to give him his just due, strove mightily when the attack fell on us, and it is largely through his efforts that any of us at all came alive out of that fight. We had broken free and were fleeing when an arrow took him in the side. We carried him away, but there was no chance to do much for his wound. He asked only, 'Are we safe away?' and when they told him we were, he said 'That much I have redeemed, then,' and he spoke no more."

"From then until now, we have been marching toward the fortress, though I understand that you have been told of the dissension among us."

"I have. Before I speak to the whole group, tell me, how many goblins are in the army marching on Harglyth-Nashwer?"

"From all the signs, there appear to be somewhere over a thousand."

Lithlannon looked grave. "And yet the walls of Harglyth-Nashwer are strong. It may be a hard fight, but we should prevail."

"It would make matters easier for Holvannon if we could slip back into the fortress somehow."

"I doubt if that is possible. Not through over a thousand goblins. And yet.... May I speak to your troops?"

He shrugged. "Speak if you will. And may you have better luck talking to them than I have had."

She looked around at them. "Well, Elves, you all know me, who I am and what I am. I have come to ask you to come back to the fortress with me, to aid Holvannon."

She paused only a moment, long enough for some of those at the edges to begin to stir. She held up a hand for quiet, though to be sure there was no actual noise yet. "I know, you have been through trying times in the last few days, and here I am asking you to go from this danger into an even greater one.

"But you know me, all of you, either in person or by reputation. I may ask severe and difficult things, but I have never asked anyone to do a thing which I was not willing to do myself, and I have never lied about how difficult a thing may be.

"And think on this. Holvannon is in the fortress of Harglyth-Nashwer, preparing to fight off the goblins, knowing that it will be a hard fight, and that the odds are so close that some slight mischance may destroy him. He does not know we are at large; for all he knows, the goblins have already destroyed us. He thinks that there are no reinforcements available to him. He thinks he has only the people inside the fort to depend upon.

"And clearly we are only a few, and our effect on the outcome of the battle may be small. None could deny that for fifty-five to consider attacking a thousand or more is foolishness on the face of it. Were we to turn our faces away from Harglyth-Nashwer and march for Arlith-ysterven, none could blame us. What could we gain besides a glorious but useless death?"

She paused, looking down. Then she looked up at them again, and her voice rang. "And yet there is a way to do something, to make a difference, and to do so without simply throwing our lives away! Listen, we have among us a few who were with us when we went into Derdrona and came back out again! We took a risk then, and we came out, not only with the prisoners the goblins had taken, but with the flail Grothrion, which had belonged to Lethrion Gyl-Farras. It is a weapon that the goblins have had reason to fear in years past, and that weapon is with us this day!

"Nor do I depend solely upon Grothrion, no matter how deadly. I have a plan whereby we may well gain success, though it be at some risk to ourselves. Will you hear my plan, or will you go home?"

Those in the inner rings of the circle were enthusiastic in their response. The sullen ones on the edges were less so, but even they agreed, though mostly because they could do nothing else with the eyes of their fellows on them. Krinneth, watching all this, told himself it would have to do, and hoped whatever plan Lithlannon had in mind was not too reckless.

Her plan sounded very simple, on the face of it. "The leader of the goblin army will have set up his own tent far enough from the fortress to be safe if the defenders were to make a sudden sally. Given that there are only a little over a thousand goblins in total, this means that he will very certainly be near to the outer edge of the goblin camp.

"If we move up quietly enough, we ought to be able to rush through to kill the goblin leader and cause them to panic."

One of the dissentient Elves spoke up. "All this sounds very well, but goblin leaders are usually well-guarded. And are we, all fifty of us, expected to overcome those guards, as well as all the other goblins who happen to be near to the leader?"

Lithlannon looked at him. "I doubt if that will be necessary. I intend for us to come unseen to the edge of the goblin army. That done, we will pick our path carefully, getting as near as possible to the leader without coming near to any others. I would hope that we might achieve our end with a shower of arrows, and we all know that goblins tend to panic easily, even the bodyguards of the leaders. When he dies, the rumour of it will race through the remaining goblins, and I doubt they will stay to dispute with us."

The Elf was not fully pleased, but Lithlannon sounded so definite, and others were casting dark looks at him, so he dared not argue further.

They set out marching.

A little less than two days later, they were at the edge of the goblin camp, concealed among the trees. They had sent out scouts ahead to check the lay of the land and the setup of the goblin camp, so that by this time they had a fair notion of how their attack would go.

They were fortunate to a degree; the goblin-chief had had his tent set up quite some distance from the walls of the fortress which, as Lithlannon had predicted, placed the tent near the outer edge of the goblin camp.

They had planned their attack to come just at evening, when there was still enough light for some archery, but when the goblins, who preferred to sleep during the day, would be not fully awake, and possibly more prone to panic.

As they watched, there was movement on the walls of the fortress. Some sort of long wooden beam sprang upright behind the wall. At the end of the beam was a wooden basket, and as the beam ceased its movement, out of the basket sprang its cargo, a mass of small stones. They seemed each to be about the size of a man's two fists, and they spread out as they flew. They arced into the air over the goblin camp, then descended, striking with a fearsome impact.

With the goblins scattered, mostly sleeping, the stones did not have the effect they might have, but they did at least disturb the sleep of many. As the Elves watched, the beam was pulled back down out of sight again. A few moments later, it sprang upright once more, launching more stones out over the goblin camp, this time in a slightly different direction.

Krinneth looked at Lithlannon. "The Facherlein, I expect."

She nodded. "Well, if we stay here very long, we are likely to be discovered, and lose all chance of surprise." She turned to the Elves.

"Now follow me and remember, we have come to fight the goblin leader, and we do not stop to fight others. Let us go!"

They did not rush forward in a shouting mass, as men might do, but rather moved forward quickly and silently, as was the habit of Elves. They rushed between the goblin tents, among the goblins bedded down on the ground, speeding quickly to their goal.

The goblin chief was apparently still in his tent, and even in the first moments when the alarm was given, he did not appear. As his bodyguards were alerted and massed to face the attack, Lithlannon shouted, "Bows!"

The Elves paused for a moment, lifted their bows, and lofted arrows into the air, aiming for the tent. Two flights of arrows riddled the tent, and it seemed unlikely anyone inside could have escaped unwounded. The next flight of arrows struck among the bodyguard, then the Elves leaped forward again.

This time they shouted as they came, shouting the old war-cries which had been heard in the many battles between Elf and goblin, and bright weapons flashed in the light of the setting sun.

Goblins are hardy and strong, skilled and fierce fighters, but prone to sudden panic without some chief or officer present to command them or rally them. Such surprises as the sudden appearance in their midst of a band of Elves was enough to frighten many into flight, even some of the officers whose duty was to rally them.

While goblin-soldiers rushed to and fro, seeking escape from the bright swords of the Elves whom rumour had multiplied greatly, the chiefs and officers, seeing how few the Elves actually were, attempted to rally them. During that same time, the Elves reached the ground occupied by the tent of the Goblin-chief and his bodyguard.

The bodyguards of goblin-chiefs are fairly large and strong and, unlike the ordinary goblin-soldiers, are not much given to panicking, and will usually guard their master until death. By the time the Elves had reached them, their officers had mustered them into formation to resist the attack, even though the Chief himself had not yet come out of the tent.

This fact would certainly tell on the goblins, as time went on, for while they would guard their Chief with their lives, there were only a few who would hold to the field after the Chief had died.

The arrows of the Elves had told heavily on the bodyguard as well, so that it was about an even match for numbers. When Grothrion struck, however, the flail's effect was noticeable. The goblins of the bodyguard, being stronger and sturdier than the ordinary soldiers, stood to face Krinneth despite his weapon. But though they fought, they also fell, and shortly the presence of the dread weapon was known throughout their ranks.

And in the meantime, their leader had not yet come out of the arrow-slashed tent, a fact which made them feel certain he was dead. A few at the rear of the formation fled, braving the weapons of their own officers who cut down deserters as willingly as they cut down enemies.

For a little while, the fight still hung in the balance, and the deserters were few. After a while, it could no longer be doubted that the Chief was either dead or dying, and even the swords of the officers could not hold the goblins in their ranks against the fierce Elves.

Throughout most of the goblin army, two rumours spread rapidly; one was the rumour of the death of the Chief, the other was the rumour of the presence of Grothrion. Most of the goblin army scattered.

But here and there were a few more sturdy ones, most of them officers, who strove to rally what troops they could. None of these groups were very large, a hundred at the most, but they advanced toward the spot where the last of the bodyguard were melting away under Elvish swords.

Krinneth was a little surprised to see that one of the officers was Shathka, the same goblin-leader against whom they had fought at Derdrona on the day when he had acquired Grothrion. Lithlannon was beside him suddenly. "We are still outnumbered, and I doubt we would survive a dash to the gates of the fortress. Best we should try to get back to the cover of the woods."

But the rallied goblins were coming up fast, and they overtook the Elves before they could reach the woods. The Elves formed into a ring and fought, a fight which seemed sure to end in disaster. Bright swords and spears flashed and struck, and goblins went down. Grothrion smote, each blow being deadly to the bodies and wills of goblins. For all that, however, there were still sufficient goblins to destroy the Elves.

There seemed no end of snarling goblin-faces, leaping against the Elf-weapons with sword, spear or axe. Most tried to avoid Grothrion, but there were even some bolder ones who offered battle to Krinneth. Despite that, the Elves were clearly in a desperate position.

But the goblins, and indeed most of the Elves, had forgotten something. There was a sudden clear call of a trumpet. The gate of Harglyth-Nashwer swung open, and Holvannon led his troops out, quickstepping in close formation across the field.

Shathka came close enough to Krinneth to snarl at him, "There will be another day!" then he turned and led his goblins from the field.

Krinneth turned to look at Lithlannon, and his smile turned to a look of concern when he saw the red stain on her leg, just above the knee.

She looked at him, looked at the wound, then smiled and tied a bit of cloth around it. Still smiling, she looked at him again. "It is nothing serious. No, truthfully, it is not serious. Would I not know, having been a healer?" She grinned at him, and he smiled back, but for all that, she leaned on his shoulder as they marched to the fort.

Holvannon was happy to see them all, for he had given them all up for lost, including the whole of the force which had gone forth under Dys-Lumyll. And he was even more happy that their return had defeated the goblins, making it very unlikely they could gather for a second attempt on his fortress.

But Krinneth saw Holvannon's expression alter slightly when he saw Lithlannon leaning on Krinneth's shoulder. For all that, though, he greeted them with all good cheer, welcoming them back as though nothing were amiss.

Chapter Nineteen
HOME ONCE MORE

Krinneth rode once more down the winding road around the mere, riding once more to Dhahal's castle. So long, so long it had been, since that first time when he had come back from being healed!

Back in Faerie, they had driven the goblins off. Seeing the real danger threaten, the folk of the outlying villages had rapidly gathered their forces and sent them to Arlith-ysterven. It had been almost too late. For even with the new troops, the Elves could not raise the siege on all of the fortresses simultaneously, and one of them had been lost altogether.

There had been recriminations over that, for Holvannon was not one to allow an opportunity to go by, wherein he could point out that he had been right all along. There were some apologies from the outlying villages, though not many, for it was as difficult for them to admit they were wrong as it was easy for Holvannon to point out how wrong they had been.

But in the end, they beat the goblins back, and that without even the necessity of a pitched battle. And for nigh a year there had been peace, without even the raids that had gone on before. Such trouble as the goblins gave was more in the matter of sneaking about in twos and threes, stealing from the outlying villages whatever they could take without being caught.

Lately, though, there had been a few armed raids, few, but enough to hint that the goblins were perhaps gaining back their strength and their will to attack the Elves.

And so had passed Krinneth's second three years in Faerie.

He now dressed in Elven clothing, though the clothes had to be specially tailored to fit his frame. Even the horse's tack was of Elven make, and Krinneth realized that his first impression among Dhahal's folk this time would be even more striking than the last.

People looked up from their work as he rode through the hamlets, as people would look up to inspect any rider coming through. But when they looked at Krinneth, most of them continued to stare.

By now, most knew the tale of Krinneth, but it had been a long time since he had last come home, and few rightly remembered him any longer. Some, seeing this figure dressed in Elven clothing, immediately realised who he must be, but others were slower, and some doubted it even when they were told.

The sentry at Dhahal's gate was a young man, and while he had heard the tale of Krinneth, he had never seen Krinneth face to face. He slanted his pike down to bar Krinneth's way.

"Who be you, and what be you wanting?"

"I am Krinneth llin Darun, and my business is with Lord Dhahal."

"Oh, aye, and for sure! You give the name of a man, and you all togged out like an Elf or something. If you have a message for the Lord, tell me and I will take it to him when my relief comes."

"It will go hard with you when your Lord finds you have kept me waiting. Call up your sergeant and ask him."

"Call up the sergeant, is it? Aye, and for sure I will, but you may not like it!"

He took a small whistle which hung round his neck and blew three sharp blasts. For a moment, nothing happened. Then in the guardroom behind him there was the sound of hurrying feet and five more men came rushing out, all carrying pikes as well. Among them was the sergeant.

"Sergeant, this fellow, Krinneth llin Darun, claims to have business with the Lord Dhahal, and does not wish to wait."

The sergeant looked Krinneth up and down, then suddenly recognized him. "Young fool!" he growled. "This is the one who went to Faerie, who comes back from time to time. And he is in favour of the Lord Dhahal for all that, and you wish to hold him here at the gate like a wandering tinker! You'll have us all for the lash!"

Then he turned to Krinneth. "Go on in, Lord. One of these lads will go along with you to see that they take care of your horse at the stables. And if it please you, Lord, forgive young Hannil; he is young, but he will learn."

Krinneth smiled. "He does his job, albeit a bit eagerly. One ought not to fault him too much for that. And as you say, he will learn."

THERE WAS A SURPRISE awaiting Krinneth that evening. When they sat down to dinner, they introduced a young man who was sitting across from Gwathlinn as Langeth, her betrothed. He was a little surprised to find that his reaction was not anger, but rather relief. And after all, he had been expecting this; she could hardly wait nine years for him, could she? Yet she was looking at him with a truculent expression, as though she were expecting him to be angry; perhaps she had thought that the understanding between them was more than something tentative, and felt that she had betrayed him somehow.

This meal, like the previous one, was somewhat strained. Dhahal eventually began the conversation, as he had the last time, but this time, he had to work harder and longer before anyone else would join in.

Afterwards, Krinneth approached Gwathlinn, more out of politeness than anything else. "A good evening to you, Gwathlinn. I hope you may be happy."

He was not sure if she had misheard him, or misunderstood his intent, but however it was, she flared into rage. "And what else was I supposed to do? Wait nine years while you were disporting yourself in

Faerie? Then you would come back to claim me as though I were some piece of baggage you had left behind before you went on your travels, I suppose? No, if I meant that little to you, you meant less to me!"

Langeth was moving forward now, as any man might move to the support of his betrothed. His expression, however, was more that of one who has carefully calculated his action so as to bring the most benefit to himself.

But Dhahal himself was at Krinneth's elbow, gripping his arm as though to restrain him. Krinneth turned toward Dhahal, who looked at him, a little diffidently. "Look you, lad, we had no formal arrangement, only a tentative one. And I could not keep Gwathlinn waiting forever, do you see?"

"You have mistaken me, Lord; I merely wanted to wish her happiness. I know that the only arrangement we had was that I should return to you again after my time of service in Faerie was done. Unless you no longer have a place for me?"

"A place for you? Krinneth, lad, there will always be a place for you here! Even after I am gone, my heir will see to that!"

AS HE RODE BACK TO Faerie, Krinneth considered the situation. Gwathlinn, as the youngest of Dhahal's daughters, had very little standing in the world. It was not Krinneth she had loved, but the thought of the position she would have as his wife. Even her concern for his wound, the concern which had driven her to take him to the Westermoor, had been mostly concern that as an invalid, he could not provide her with the position she desired. For that, she was willing to pay any price, even urging him to make his agreement with Lithlannon before asking the consent of Dhahal, to whom he had owed prior allegiance.

And when it turned out that Krinneth was not willing to break his word to Lithlannon, and that he would be away for nine years before they could be wed, Gwathlinn grew angry. And of course, when another opportunity arose, she would put aside her unofficial arrangement with Krinneth to grasp at the new chance offered to her. As for Krinneth, well, he had three more years yet to go before he need concern himself with the matter. And again, he felt somehow relieved that he need not concern himself with Gwathlinn.

Chapter Twenty
THE SHIELD AGAIN

The King was sitting on his throne again, looking much the same as he had the previous time. Michmesh was sitting beside him again, and the Puchlein raised his small cup in a salute to Krinneth.

"You are well, Krinneth?" asked the King.

"Quite well, thank you."

"And you, Lithlannon? You are quite well?"

"Quite well, thank you." She smiled at him. "Would I be correct in suspecting that you have another task for us?"

The King chuckled. "Do I never call you except to send you out on errands? Surely you will not say that!"

"Perhaps it only seems so," she answered.

"And if we did not occasionally send you out on errands, would you not merely find other occasions to do mischief?" He sat up straighter then, a signal the time for joking was done. "We have heard some interesting news from Michmesh, and it seemed best to me that the two of you should hear it at once. Michmesh?"

The Puchlein set down his small cup then smiled. "There are being many wild folk in the hills, folk who be wandering the wilds and not gathering to the towns. We Puchlein are meeting such from time to time in our own wanderings and are passing news and tidings from one to another.

"Most recently, a tale has been coming down, from many folk, of an ogre who is walking the hills, bearing a shield set with strange stones. Now, from one or from two, this tale might be being set aside as tales being told to impress, but from many, it is seeming less likely so. And there are some telling the tale whose truthfulness we would not be questioning."

"And thus I am coming to be telling you about all this, that you may be knowing and making your own decisions."

Before the King or anyone else could speak, Krinneth said, "What of the goblins? Can we afford to send anyone away at this time?"

"We believe so," said the King. "The only word we hear from them is that they are preparing for war, but are far from ready yet. And besides that, we are not in the situation we were several years ago, with our armies weakened nearly to the point of ineffectiveness. The folk of the outlying villages have learned their lesson, and the contingents are coming in more regularly now."

Krinneth nodded, then spoke. "If I understand matters aright, you will wish us to go off hunting for this ogre who carried the shield."

"That is in my mind. Mostly I asked that you come to be consulted. Michmesh, what say you? Is it likely to be possible to hunt this one ogre and find him?"

Michmesh shrugged. "For certain and for certain, it is not possible to be telling. Most of the stories are telling of him wandering a particular part of the Hills, which would seem to be suggesting that if one is going into that area, he might be finding the ogre."

"And what do you say, Lithlannon?"

"Will you come with us, Michmesh?"

"For certain, for certain! If you are going, I shall be going with you."

"Only the three of us?" inquired Krinneth. "Or can you spare us a few more warriors? If this is wild country, as I understand it to be, we may need help."

Quarannon smiled. "No, I would not send you on such a task without help or aid. Would twenty warriors suffice?"

Krinneth looked at Lithlannon, who looked back at him and nodded. "Twenty will certainly suffice; indeed, more might be too many. But we will have none of your youngsters barely learning the trade of the warrior; we must have all warriors proven and able, Elves who can live in the wild without complaint, and who are thoroughly capable."

The King nodded. "Our commanders will not like to see their best whistled away on such a quest, when it is clear that the goblin raids are beginning again. But I can see that for this task you will need the best, no matter who complains."

Krinneth spoke up then. "There seems no doubt that this shield is the very shield we seek. If that is so, why have they not already used it against us?"

The King smiled wryly. "There may be a number of reasons for that. The shield may indeed be one of those things which displays its full ability only for the Elves, and so far as the ogre is concerned, he carries only a shield, though it be very decorated.

"And on the other hand, since it is an ogre that carries the shield at present, he may well know and use its ability, but may not have any sort of following with which to use it against us.

"I suspect the former, however, for if its power was manifest for the ogre, he would surely by now have made himself more important among the ogres, perhaps even replacing Hoodaldow himself."

The flying machine of the Facherlein had changed mightily from its first appearance. Not only were the wings very different, with attached rods and pulleys and cords to change their shape while they beat, but a tail had also been added, a tail in the general form of a kite, fabric stretched over thin rods. In addition, they had installed a sort of revolving fan apparatus in the front, apparently turned by the same steam which powered the wings.

As in the other tests, as the steam built up, the wings beat ferociously, and at the same time, the fan also began to revolve rapidly. The machine hopped forward, each hop taking it a little further than the last, until it hopped off the edge of the table. An instant before it could hit the floor, it righted itself slightly and actually began to fly. It climbed somewhat as it flew, causing the Elves to scramble out of its path, and clearing the next table by a scant finger-breadth.

Gathering momentum, the machine hurtled onward, smoke and steam pouring from it to end by smashing against the wall of the hall. Some young Elf had the presence of mind to rush forward and pour water on it, putting out the fire and sending up hissing clouds of smoke and steam.

The three gnomes paid little attention to all this. They were shaking hand among themselves, smiling broadly, and chattering together, congratulating themselves for the fact that the machine had flown, and discussing what must be done to make it fly even better.

Chapter Twenty-One
INTO THE WILD COUNTRY

Krinneth knew for certain they were coming into the wild country. During the first days, there were small villages or farms of the Elves here and there, but these had become fewer and fewer until today, when they had walked from sunup to sundown without any sign of settlement.

They had seen no sign of goblins either, for which they were well-pleased. The whole purpose of their trip was not particularly to engage in fighting, though they were all resigned to some sort of fight at the end; after all, it was not likely the ogre would meekly give up the shield to them. On the other hand, the less fighting they did now, the more likely they would be ready and able for that fight when it came.

The Elves in their band were all seasoned warriors, tried and tested in many battles. There had been some concern about taking even this few away from the Elvish armies at a time when they expected a renewal of the goblin attacks at any moment. On the other hand, the quest for the Shield was also vital, and it had come down to balancing the possibility of the recovery of the Shield against the absence of twenty warriors.

They moved silently through the woods, passing unseen among the trees. Krinneth himself had learned many of the tricks of the Elves for going and coming without being marked, though he knew he was by no means as skilled as any of these. He was capable enough, however, and he was always willing to learn, for which the others were at least willing to accept him.

The Facherlein trailed along at the back of the line. For all their heavy packs and paraphernalia, they too moved quickly and quietly along the trail. He still could not find out exactly why they insisted on trailing along with him. When he asked them bluntly, they gave long and evasive answers, answers which sounded quite reasonable until he had time to think about them, at which time he discovered they had told him nothing at all except that the idea seemed good to them.

And after all, they were no extra trouble, and though they were constantly involved with the building and making of strange devices, they took their turn with the camp work, and were quite able to carry their weight. He therefore let them be. He knew that among the other members of the party there were various attitudes, but most of them had sufficient respect for the ability and good sense of Lithlannon that they did not question what she would allow.

At the thought of Lithlannon, he frowned. He had come into Faerie to pay a debt, and he still had obligations in the world outside. The hold on him was the same, even though there was no longer any question of an arrangement with Gwathlinn. It was not Gwathlinn but his own faith, which would draw him back, promises and oaths sworn to Dhahal.

At that moment Lithlannon stopped, pointed at the ground, and said something in a quiet voice. They passed the word down the line until it got to him "Goblin-trail crossing ours," said the Elf in front of him. "probably a week old. Maybe thirty goblins."

Krinneth nodded and passed the word back behind him. If the trail were a week old, and crossing theirs, it was of no immediate concern to them. Of course, the goblins might have gone any direction once they crossed the trail, so it was best to be careful.

He wondered who these goblins might be, and why they would be here in this part of the country, especially during these times when it was suspected that Shtavrak was gathering all his forces. But of course, not every goblin owed allegiance to the King of Goblins, so this band might have many reasons for being here. All the same, there was a possibility that the Goblins had gotten word of the Shield and had sent a force of their own to seek it.

They discussed the matter among themselves that evening, and concluded that given what else wandered the hills, thirty goblins hardly increased the danger. And as for the fear the goblins might themselves be seeking the Shield, the consensus was that they had come to get the Shield, expecting to fight to take it, and the thought of having to fight to keep it was not really so unexpected. And if the goblins got the Shield first, and the Elves were forced to take it from them, well, that would be only a different sort of battle.

That being settled, they then went on to their usual nightly pursuit of telling tales and singing old songs, which they would do just before settling down for a night's sleep. One song being sung that night was 'The Lord is away in the forest.'

"*O come to me knights, and come hither warriors;*
Come forth with your sword and your sharp, shining spear.
For battle is threatening, our homes are in peril;
For the Dark Elves are marching, their hosts have come near,
And your Lord is away in the forest.
O lady, my lady, the foe are attacking,
They bend their black bows and assail our walls.
Go down, now, we pray you, lest harm should come to you,
Go down and be sheltered within our high hall,
Till our Lord shall come home from the forest.
Let them come with their swords, let them come with their arrows,
I will not go down, I will not hide away.
I will stay here above and keep the wall with you,
With sword in my hand with the warriors I stay,
For our Lord is away in the forest.
O lady, my lady, O woe now betide us!
There is blood on your hand and blood on your breast!

A swift-flying arrow or bright sword has found you;
Go down from the wall that your wound may be dressed.
For our Lord is away in the forest.
I am struck by the bright-darting blade, I am wounded.
Down from the high wall unwilling I go.
Fight on and fight fiercely, do not be disheartened,
As our numbers lessen, our spirit shall grow.
Till our Lord shall come home from the forest.
The walls had been taken, and dear was the taking,
And down in the courtyard a shield-ring still fought;
Encircling the lady whose memory they honoured,
Fighting grimly and fiercely, for life caring not,
When the Lord came at last from the forest."

As the singer completed the song, Krinneth suddenly found his mind was far away, thinking once more of his situation. He was rapidly brought back to the present when Lithlannon herself dropped down beside him.

"And what deep, dark thoughts are you thinking to make your brow so black?"

He shrugged. "This and that, this and that."

She grinned at him. "Worse than I thought. 'This and that' are some of the most terrible things to have on your mind. Tell me, what is your 'this and that?'"

He shrugged. She looked at him closely.

"Perhaps you feel I have no right to ask these things of you. Yet I lead this party, and if one of the party is in any way unhappy with the way it is being led, or with the quest itself, then I must be concerned. There are few enough of us, and if any unspoken concerns hinder the ability of one of us, it puts the rest of us in danger."

He looked at her. "Perhaps it is only foolishness, but perhaps you should know." He went on to explain what had been bothering him, his concern for what he ought to do when his time in Faerie was done.

"The two of us," he concluded, "have been coming closer and closer, because we have been working together so often. Yet I have ties in the world outside. I have commitments back with Westermoor as much as here. And though I would be willing to take you with me, what then? If you were willing to leave this land you love so much, what could I offer you? A standing not of the highest, nor yet of the lowest, with people everywhere making signs against you to ward off evil magic. Myself they might eventually accept, since I was once one of them, but I fear you would be always an outsider and stranger. I would not have you suffer that, you see? And so I do not wish to seem to promise you more than I can give."

She spoke more quietly then. "So be it, then."

She was about to get up and leave, and he could see the heaviness of her heart. "Lithlannon?" She looked at him. "Lithlannon, I must be here in Faerie for some time yet. Can we not be friends and comrades for that time?"

She smiled and sat down again. "Having done what we have done and suffered what we have suffered together, we can hardly be less. And let the future hold what it may hold!"

They clasped hands, then, and it was all Krinneth could do to remember his resolve of moments ago, that he would remember his commitments in the world outside, whatever happened.

They travelled further into the wild country. They still sang and told tales in the evening, but they were much more careful now. From time to time they saw strange things in the night, things which could affright even the hardiest Elf. They suffered no attacks, however, save for when they came upon a young wyvern unawares. If they had not surprised it, it would likely have fled at their coming. As it was, they had a few minutes of hard fighting before they could get back under the trees where the beast could not come, and several of them suffered minor wounds.

Occasionally, in the evenings, Michmesh would leave the camp and be gone until near morning. When they inquired, he beamed. "Off getting news, for certain, for certain! The small folk who are knowing all the news of the wild, they are not willing to come near to so many large folk. So it is I myself who must be going out seeking for them, to be finding the news and bringing it back."

All he could find, though, were rumours and tales, mostly some weeks old, and many from far away. And all they could do was guess at which direction they should go, and continue travelling.

From time to time, they saw signs of goblins, but they were always a few days or weeks old. It was impossible to tell with traces so old, whether there were many bands of goblins, or possibly just one. They discussed this at times around the fire in the evening. They agreed there were probably several bands of goblins. Whether they were specifically seeking something, or whether they were merely wandering about in search of whatever they could find in the way of loot or slaves, could not yet be determined.

They continued to wander the hills, following up whatever slim clues Michmesh could find. The ogre would be reported to be in a particular place, so they would go to that place. When they got there, however, they found the report had been mistaken, or the ogre had long ago moved on, and no one had any idea where he had gone.

Then one drizzly afternoon, they came upon a centaur battling with a band of goblins. The centaur was armed with a large club, and used his hooves effectively as well. But for all that, there were about thirty attackers, and he was not able to guard himself from all directions. He was already bleeding from several slight wounds, and eventually those wounds would slow him sufficiently so that one goblin could wound him seriously, and the end would come quickly after that.

Lithlannon looked from the fight to her small band and back, then simply said, "Come."

With no further command needed, the Elves descended on the goblins in wrath.

The goblins probably never knew how many or how few the Elves were. One moment they were having their rough amusement with the centaur, the next they were being attacked by grim Elves. Five of them died in the first instant before they were aware of being attacked at all. Several more were slain in the next instant before they could reform to meet the attack, and several others as the band took to its heels and fled.

Krinneth looked around and noted that none of the Elves had taken more hurt than a scratch or two. He saw Lithlannon was also surveying her party to see who was hurt. The others were also seeing who of their companions were wounded, and wrapping up the worst scratches with whatever was at hand. They then turned to the centaur.

He spoke to them in the Elvish language, though his speech was so strongly accented so that some of his words could not be understood immediately. "Ha good day to you, Elffen Folkh. Hit was honly chust in time that you did come. You have my gratitude, hiff that matters to you hat hall."

"We would likely have done the same for any creature under attack by goblins," answered Lithlannon. "My name is Lithlannon, and I lead this party."

"My name his Khorin, hand Hi ffoolishly hallowed myselff to be separated ffrom my band. Hwe had not hitherto been haware hof khoblins hin the near vicinity."

"We have seen traces of goblins from time to time in the last few weeks. Do they not usually come into these parts, then?"

As Lithlannon spoke, some Elves approached Khorin with bandages. He shied away from them for a moment, then saw what they intended and held still.

"Hennh, there hare halways ha ffew hof them. Hin recent times, though, there have been more, hin bands such has this. Halways khoblins hare troublemakers, but these hare heven more troublesome."

"Do they seek for something, do you know?"

"Hi cannot say. Perhaps. Hand perhaps they have merely been fforced hout hof khoblin territory down below, so they hafflict hus."

Lithlannon nodded. "What of ogres? Have you seen or heard aught of ogres?"

The centaur's face took on a wary expression. "Some, some. Hwhat hwould you know?"

"There is a certain ogre of whom we have heard rumours. He bears a special shield."

"That hwone! Hi know honly hwhat Hi have heard, you hunderstand? But they say he his more trouble hin the hills than ha hundred khoblins."

"Do you know where he is to be found?"

Khorin shrugged, a shrug which started with the shoulders and rippled down over his whole body. "Hwhen last Hi heard, he hwas hwell to the hwest hof here. But he moves, he moves. He has probably not come closer, hor Hi hwould have heard hit."

"Thank you, Khorin. That information is at least as good as the information we have been following so far. We will go west."

Again, there was that rippling shrug. Khorin smiled as he spoke. "No, hit his Hi hwo must thankh you, Lithlannon. Hi live, hwhen Hi hought to have died. Ha saffe chourney to you, hand may you come saffe home, hagain."

Chapter Twenty-Two
LOST TRAILS AND SCANT NEWS

They discussed the situation thoroughly. "Some of the goblin-shields bear the symbols of Shtavrak," Lithlannon declared. "This suggests that he sent them out on some errand. And we all remember how King Quarannon thought long and hard before he sent us out. Surely Shtavrak will have had similar thoughts, and would not send his warriors on any casual errand into the hills. I fear he has heard of the Shield, and wishes to have it for himself, or at the very least, keep it out of our hands."

"What do we do, then? Surely there are sufficient of us that we need not fear thirty goblins?" spoke up one of the Elves.

"Indeed not, if it were only thirty goblins. But the best trackers among us cannot say that all the tracks we have seen have been made by the same band of goblins. Goblins have always been more numerous than Elves, and it is not at all unlikely that three, four, or more bands are travelling these hills on the same errand as we ourselves. That being so, it is almost certain that our paths shall cross from time to time."

Another Elf spoke. "But Shtavrak and Hoodaldow are allies. If Shtavrak is aware of the Shield and its importance, why does he not approach his ally and ask for it?"

Lithlannon smiled. "The goblins and the ogres may be allies, but that does not mean that they trust each other completely. From what I know of Hoodaldow, if he were aware of the Shield and its importance, he would very likely try to sell it to the Elves for some great price, whereas Shtavrak is more likely to want to keep it from us at all, since his overwhelming desire is to destroy us. And I suspect that Shtavrak knows his ally at least as well as I, and therefore he will keep his knowledge to himself if he can.

"But that is not really our present problem. We have to decide how much risk we are willing to take to recover the Shield."

Krinneth, who had been mostly listening, put in his opinion. "If the goblins are searching for the Shield, is it not more important than ever that we should find it, and find it first?"

"Ah!" said Lithlannon. "Now that is the situation put clearly! If Shtavrak is searching for the Shield, does that not mean that we ought to take more risks to recover it sooner?"

After a little more discussion, they decided it was important to keep the Shield out of the hands of the goblins, and so they would continue their search. One of their number was able to lure down a bird and send a message to the King telling of the news and their decision to carry on with the quest.

But for all the new resolve, there was little result. They went westward, as the centaur had suggested, but they did not find the ogre. They found old traces showing that ogres had been in the vicinity, but nothing recent. Michmesh, after spending a night out seeking for news, came back with his smile slightly less broad.

"Little news for certain, for certain. An ogre had been stopping here, had been staying near, but he is being gone long ago, perhaps back down to the lowlands, but no one is knowing for certain. There are being stories of goblins, though, goblins wandering the hills and acting as goblins always do, killing and maiming for no good reason, save that it is being the goblin way."

So again they quartered the hills, seeking any sign of the ogres. Such traces, as they discovered, were mostly old, and the news they heard was never clear. The ogres had been there; they had gone; the ogres had come and had a massive battle with an army of Elves and had been driven away. The ogres had had a massive battle and had driven the Elves away. The ogres had gone back to the lowlands for reinforcements.

"I am thinking," said Michmesh regarding these last stories, "that word of our battle with the goblins is being confused with the presence of the ogres, and much being made of it."

"I think so too," said Lithlannon. "But this story of the ogres having gone away, what of that? Perhaps it is true."

The Puchlein shrugged his tiny winged shoulders. "Perhaps and perhaps. Sometimes I may be distinguishing truth from invention, sometimes not. If we should be allowing the facts to be influencing us, then possibly the very absence of ogres might be saying to us that they are being long gone. And yet..." he trailed off, with another expressive shrug.

It was not quite a complete surprise, therefore, when they came upon a group of ogres the next day.

It was evening when the scouts reported the ogres, five of them, gathered around a small fire where they were eating their evening meal. The scouts had not specifically seen the Shield Set with Onyx, but there were several weapons and bits of armour about, and this band of ogres seemed more organized than usual.

Lithlannon looked around at her small band. "I suppose, then, that the only thing to do is to accost them and ask after our property."

"Accost them?" asked one of the Elves, as though not quite believing his ears. "Accost a band of ogres? For myself, I would prefer not to give them warning at all."

"And I fully understand, Rhigannon. I feel sure it will come to a fight no matter what we do, and yet this is not our land, even if it is not theirs, and to simply attack without warning smacks of banditry, if not outright goblinishness.

"But I had not meant to do anything so foolish as to wander into their camp with weapons sheathed, and trust to their good nature. Here is my plan."

KRINNETH WAS BECOMING a little uneasy. Surely the other Elves must have found their places by now? Or had they met with some difficulty? Ogres were not really masters of silent movement in the forest, nor were they in the habit of having roving sentries guarding their camp, but something must have happened, or the signal would have been given by now.

He looked over at Lithlannon. But she was sitting quietly, as though she had no worries. She even looked up and caught his glance and smiled. Was she not worried? Did she not think that it was time and past time they did something?

But he was not about to press her. She was no tyro. She had fought and scouted before, and if she felt that the time was not too long, then the time was not too long. Or was it?

Then a bird-call sounded from across the clearing. She looked up at Krinneth again and smiled, as though she knew just what he had been thinking. She pursed her lips and made an answering call, he could see her lips move as she counted off:

"One in the forest,
Two on the hill,
Three by the brookside..."

Instead of counting four, she stepped out into the clearing, Krinneth stepping with her. At the same time, with hardly a sound, the other Elves had stepped out as well, all of them with bows drawn, standing in a great circle around the ogres. Michmesh was a little in front of Krinneth and Lithlannon, his own tiny bow drawn as well.

The ogres had noticed nothing at first, then suddenly one of them gave an exclamation, and they were all grasping for weapons.

"Hold!" shouted Lithlannon. "If we had come to slay you, we should have done so without your seeing us. We have come to ask for information. There is no need for fighting."

One ogre, who was slightly taller than the others, answered. His command of the Elvish language was not at all complete, but he could make himself understood. "Elves want talk? Fear fight?"

"We do not fear to fight. As I said, we want information, and a fight would do neither of us any good."

"Hah! In-for-mation, is it? No, in-for-mation here, pretty Elf, only ogres. And we claim this territory in the name of Malbalgrin the Mighty and Hoodaldow, the Ogre Lord. So best you should be off."

Lithlannon shook her head. "No, not without what we have come for. We need to know of an ogre who bears—-"

She got no further. Perhaps the ogre thought that the Elves, seeking information, would be a little slow to loose their arrows, and that by attacking in the midst of the parley he could take them by surprise. However, it was. He gave a shout and charged for Lithlannon. His fellows followed behind him, brandishing weapons.

But the Elves were not caught completely by surprise. These were all veterans, experienced warriors, and the ogres had barely begun to move when the first arrows were loosed.

Three ogres fell to the first flight of arrows, and the other two were wounded. The Elves each nocked another arrow, but by the time they were drawing their bows, they did not dare loose for fear of hitting Lithlannon or Krinneth, each of whom had loosed a second arrow.

The leader of the ogres continued, coming so close neither of the two could loose another arrow, but his fellow fell, strove to rise again, then slumped down. Lithlannon skipped back away from the ogre, drawing her sword, while Krinneth pulled Grothrion free from his belt. At the same instant, he saw a tiny arrow strike the ogre's thigh, and knew Michmesh had got off one more shot.

And just as he was stepping in to swing the flail, the ogre-leader stumbled, went to one knee, got both feet under him again, and toppled forward like a great tree.

The Elves spent a little time checking to be sure that the ogres were dead, then looked over their belongings. It was a disappointing lot. Aside from the usual rough ogre swords, spears, and knives, there were only two shields. One was crudely woven out of wicker, the other was a couple of planks of oak bound together by wooden bracing, and roughly carved into a more or less circular shape. Some iron strapping was added around the rim, and a boss of metal in the center, but that was all.

Lithlannon shook her head, and turned to Michmesh. "Michmesh, is it at all possible that anyone could have mistaken either of these for the Shield Set with Onyx? You know your sources of information better than any of us."

The Puchlein considered both the shields, frowned, then shook his head. "No, I am thinking not. The Shield was being described, down to the exact form of the onyx plates upon its surface. I am doubting that any one, even the most impressionable of the Small Folk, could be making such a mistake."

Lithlannon rubbed a hand on her chin. "I thought not. And it is not at all unlikely that there could be two or more bands of ogres wandering the hills. So," She looked around at the others. "Let us camp here for a time, and let Michmesh see what he can find out. I doubt if these are the ogres we have been seeking, but we shall see."

The news which Michmesh eventually brought back was more positive than they had hoped for. "It is seeming that this band of ogres which we were just meeting were being part of a larger band, led by the one bearing the Shield. The group was separating here, with this lot waiting here, camping in various places in the neighbourhood, while the others were leaving. Some are saying that the rest were going back down to the lowlands, to be bringing more ogres to be making a settlement. Others say that they have been going farther north to be doing more exploring."

Chapter Twenty-Three
MABALGRIN THE MIGHTY

It did not become immediately apparent that they were on a false trail. As Michmesh explained, "One is not being able merely to ask for news, else one must be listening to long lists of trials, of the failing of this mushroom crop or the disappearing of that berry, and so on. So one must ask if they are knowing anything of a band of ogres. Some will be saying truthfully enough that they are knowing nothing, others will be retailing little bits that they have been hearing elsewhere, and oftentimes making them a little better by adding of embellishments. So one must be taking in all the stories, then testing them in one's mind to be seeing whether they might be being true, or being products of invention. And this is never being easy."

For two weeks, they worked their way north, always teased by rumours that the ogres had been in this place just recently, but had gone away, and there was a choice of directions in which they might have gone. There were also always stories of goblins and the atrocities they were committing.

Suddenly, they were getting a new rumour. The ogres were building a fortress to the south. "They are?" questioned Lithlannon. "Ogres, building a fortress? I said it was unlikely when first we heard it, you recall. It does not seem more likely now. And yet..." she scowled as she brooded. "Is there any way to test the truth of this story, save by going back?"

Michmesh shrugged. "Probably not. But I can be telling you one thing for certain, for certain. This story has been travelling up from the south during the last day or two. It is being newer than any of the stories we have been hearing so far, which may or may not be making it more likely to be being true."

"So." Lithlannon sat in thought for a long while, then finally got up. "We will go north one more day, and if we do not hear any fresher or better news, then we will start south again. I suppose there are stranger things happening in the world than ogres building a fortress."

In the night, a bird came to them.

The bird brought tidings from the King himself. The goblins were gathering again, and there had already been a few small raids on Elvish settlements. This time, though, the Elves were much better prepared and had more warriors to send out to the fight. The King also acknowledged receipt of their message and bade them be alert. If the goblins were indeed seeking the Shield, it would be good for the Elves to know at least that much.

With the knowledge the goblins appeared to be once more ready to make war, and that their quest was more urgent than ever, they set out to the south.

The party took their northward trek fairly slowly, stopping here and there to let Michmesh go out and seek information. They hurried a little on the return journey, considering that the news they might pick up would not have changed a great deal. They continued to hear recent stories about the fortress of the ogres. Depending upon who was telling the story, it was a rough work of logs, a fence built of carefully squared planks, with fine buildings inside, and protected by spells, or a fine work of stones, tall and mighty, one which would prove a trial to the doughtiest of warriors. Then there were various and sundry embellishments on these themes, but the underlying story appeared to be certain.

As a result of their hurrying, they were in the neighbourhood of their meeting with the ogres some three and a half weeks after they had set out. Michmesh could then get some more accurate information regarding the site of the ogres' building endeavours, and they moved in that direction with a good deal of caution.

They found it at last, and all of them were impressed, particularly those most familiar with ogres and their works.

A large clearing was found in the woods. This clearing was being made larger by the labour of ogres with large axes. Within the clearing, they had erected a large palisade, a palisade of huge logs, bound together and braced against falling, and sharpened at the tip to dissuade intruders. Within the palisade a walkway had been built around the wall, so sentries could march about and keep watch.

There were also buildings inside the palisade, something strange for ogres indeed. Roofs of several houses were visible, and they estimated there were somewhere upward of fifty ogres in the fortress.

"Well," said Michmesh. "They are being found at last, for certain, for certain."

"We have found ogres, it is true. But is the Shield here?"

The Puchlein shrugged. "I will be asking this night. In the meantime, though, we can be keeping watch and seeing what we may be seeing."

As it turned out, Michmesh did not need to ask that night. The Elves kept watch, and eventually, they saw an ogre carrying a shield. One of the Elves touched Lithlannon on the sleeve and pointed.

"There! See that one with the shield? Does it not seem too small for him, as though it were built more for one of our size?"

"It does seem so, but let us try to look closer. More than one ogre might be carrying a plundered shield."

But eventually the ogre came near enough that they could see the shield and have no doubt. It was the Shield Set with Onyx.

Lithlannon made signals to them, and they slipped away from the clearing. When they had reached what they thought was a safe distance, they made camp. After they had eaten, Lithlannon spoke what was on the minds of most of them. "So, the Shield is there indeed. Now, how do we take it from the midst of so many ogres?"

There was much discussion on this point. Everyone realized a raid was out of the question, heavily outnumbered as they were. This left two alternatives; wait and watch to catch the ogre outside the fort for a time when he was less well-guarded, or to send a small party to slip into the fort by night and take the Shield by stealth.

After everyone had spoken, Lithlannon stood. "This will be no simple matter," she said. "If we wait to catch the ogre unawares, we may have a long wait. You will have noticed that he bears a guard of five wherever he goes, and there are usually a few others hanging about. Any attack we make risks that those five will keep up a fight long enough for others to rally.

"Further, the longer we stay about, waiting for the proper circumstances, the greater the chance that we will be discovered by an ogre or ogres, either scout, working party, or chance wanderer. If that happens, they may well draw us into a battle willy-nilly.

"And recall our meeting with the band of five? They have certainly had some connection with this group, and their failure to join the main body will be noted. There will be at least suspicion in the minds of the ogres that enemies are abroad, and they will thus be more watchful.

"As for slipping into the fort by night, that is a possibility. But we would have to know first what the fort is like inside, and that requires some scouting. Michmesh, would you be able to slip into the fort unseen?"

"Need you be asking?" a touch of scorn was heard in the voice of the Puchlein. "The day I am not being able to elude a gang of clumsy ogres, I ought to be setting my bow aside and preparing my grave!"

There was a protest by one of the Elves that the Puchlein should go and do their scouting for them. Was there no Elf capable of such work?

"Indeed, there are, and any one of us might be able to do this. But because of his size, Michmesh has much the better chance of doing so and remaining undetected. And this is not a matter of showing off skill, this is a matter of laying groundwork for an important task."

She turned back to Michmesh. "Can you make this attempt tonight? As I have said, the longer we wait here, the more dangerous our situation is."

Michmesh bowed. "It will be done, then, this very night."

That evening, shortly after dark, Michmesh slipped out of the camp quietly. The Elves waited, with a brief show of impatience, for his return. Singing was seldom around the campfire that night. A few old stories were told, but in general, they merely sat and waited, and after a time, went to sleep.

Michmesh was back before they woke. He had slipped in without bothering the sentries, and was sitting at the remains of the fire having a little bite to eat. They had long since ceased to berate sentries for not noticing his comings and goings.

The first one to notice him immediately went to wake Lithlannon, and there was a sufficient stir in the camp thereafter to wake anyone else who still slept. As a result, nearly everyone was present when Michmesh gave his account of the night's work.

"The getting over the wall was not being difficult; one of my size is often not being noticed, and indeed is often being mistaken for a bird. Once over the wall, I was spending some time in the shadows noticing the way the guards were being posted, how they were walking their rounds, and the like.

"I was hearing some of them talk. They are being greatly in fear of their leader, whose name is being Mabalgrin the Mighty, and who is apparently having such influence with Hoodaldow as to be gaining permission to come up here and set up his own hold. Hoodaldow may be hoping to be removing a disruptive influence from his court.

"After a bit, I was moving around myself, seeking to find out how the fort was being set up inside. Running north to south along the east wall is a large building, a house and shelter for the guards. There is being another building along the south wall, which is appearing to be a kitchen and dining hall. In the northwest corner is another large building, apparently a storehouse.

"Midway between this storehouse and the kitchen is being a slightly smaller building, for which I was not at first divining a purpose. It was being well-guarded, with three armed ogres at its door always, and another pair ever walking in rounds about it.

"After some time, I began to realize that the thing most valuable to the chief ogre was being his own skin. Also, ogres are of the sort that a leader must ever be fearing the jealousy of one of his followers. Therefore, this is where the chief of the ogres lives.

"I was creeping closer, seeking if perhaps there might be a window through which to enter. There was, but when I was attempting to open it, I was discovering that the ogre chief is not trusting even his guards altogether. Hooked to the window are several little thongs, each fastened to a row of small bells. Moving the window is thus moving the bells, causing them to be jingling, and waking the ogre."

He looked around. "For a band to be coming in and taking the ogre-chief unawares will not be easy, for certain, for certain."

Lithlannon was considering all this. "How if we made a swift raid? Cause a disturbance over on one side of the fort to distract them, then send in five or ten on the other side."

"The sentries around the leader's quarters?" asked Krinneth.

"We come up quickly. Shoot them with arrows before they can give the alarm."

"If the disturbance we will use distracts them at all, it is likely also to wake the leader. What then?"

She frowned suddenly. "Ah, you are right, you are right! And yet, there must be a way. If we go over the walls without a distraction, we are likely to be seen before we are ready. And yet..."

For some time then they considered plans and possibilities, each one being put aside as having too many dangers attached to it. They ate their morning meal, still attempting to develop plans.

A little later in the morning, one of their scouts came rushing into camp calling out, "A band of ogres is approaching!"

There was no panic or dismay; these were all experienced warriors, and they calmly got their kit together and prepared their weapons. Lithlannon asked the scout, "Is their leader with them?"

"No. There are about twenty of them, led by one of the leader's bodyguards."

"Then we will not stay to fight. Sheathe your swords, all of you. If the leader is not with them, it is not worth the risk of lives to fight them. We will leave."

These were all experienced veterans, so there was only a small grumble of protest at this, but they followed her orders. Shortly they were leaving the campsite, moving at a quick march.

Krinneth looked back. There was little sign that anyone had been in that clearing, though it was difficult to hide the signs of the campfire. Those signs would probably alert the ogres, who might then pursue, but Elves could easily outdistance ogres over a long trail, particularly with the start they were being given.

Chapter Twenty-Four
THE LIFTING OF THE SHIELD

Once the ogres discovered that there were Elves in the neighbourhood, they became very careful. They would send out large patrols all around the fortress, so that three times they forced the Elves to flee. They still could not come up with a better plan for recovering the Shield than a quick raid by night, hoping to carry out their task before the ogres could notice their presence.

IN THE MEANTIME, THEY received another message from the King; the goblins were on the move once more.

Lithlannon finally said, "We will stay away from the fortress for two weeks. Perhaps their vigilance will ebb; and we dare not wait too long if war is afoot in the lowlands."

No one dared to ask what would happen if the vigilance of the ogres did not ebb. They all knew the answer; a raid, whatever the cost.

Michmesh was better able than the Elves to go scouting with the ogres about; even if they saw him, they would not necessarily suspect anything, for everyone knew the woods were full of Puchlein. They could not ask too much of him, for even he would grow weary if he were scouting every day. However, he helped considerably in keeping them out of the way of the ogres.

Then suddenly, they received a message from Holvannon. He asked that they set a place and a time, within three days, for a meeting. There were limits to what messages could be born by birds, but even so, this was extremely terse. "What has happened?" wondered Lithlannon. "What of the fort he was commanding? Is the war won already? But surely we would have heard word from the King if that were so."

"You realize the meaning of all this?" asked Krinneth.

"Yes, I suppose so. In the absence of any other answer, Holvannon's fort has been taken, and he has fought his way free with a few others. Finding themselves cut off from the city, they have come up to join us. I suppose that the only way to find out the truth is to meet him."

So they sent a message to Holvannon, wherever he might be, to tell him where to meet them, then they themselves marched toward the chosen place. They arrived first and set up a camp, then waited.

Toward evening of the next day, Holvannon and twenty-three Elves came quietly out of the woods into their camp. Holvannon was even more grim than Krinneth had ever seen him. The Elves with him were a lean, hard lot, who had clearly seen a battle recently, and a good deal of rough living since. Without hesitation, Lithlannon ordered food prepared for them immediately. Her own group, without argument, prepared to share their own small stocks of food with the newcomers.

Lithlannon did not press him, but shortly Holvannon said, "You will want to know what has happened, why we are here?"

"If you wish to tell us."

He nodded shortly. "Shtavrak," he began, "made his plans carefully this time. They descended upon us swiftly, and in significant force. This time they did not divide their forces between several points, but rather struck, if I am correct, at three of the fortresses.

"They swarmed up our walls, and we beat them back. The first time it was not too difficult, even the second time we threw them back and were still confident of our ability. But they came again and again, before we could recover our breath, and soon we could tell that we were losing too many to be able to hold much longer.

"We decided to take a risk; we would certainly not be able to hold the fort for much longer, and indeed holding the fort was rather a meaningless gesture, since they could easily hold us besieged while their main force went round us toward Arlith-ysterven.

"So we who were left made a sortie, which surprised the goblins who knew our situation almost as well as we did. We cut our way through and went on. They pursued us, hoping to keep us from the city, and since we knew we had little hope of evading them in that direction, we came in this one.

"What of yourselves? Have you had any luck with the finding of the Shield?"

"We have found the Shield," affirmed Lithlannon. "But the ogre who has it is in charge of a force of about a hundred others, and they have built themselves a fortress."

"Ogres building a fortress? Do you jest, Lithlannon?"

"I only wish I did. And to tell the truth, I did not believe it at first either, not until we saw the fortress."

"So, what do you plan to do?"

"We have no proper plan as yet. Our choices, to send a small party over the wall in secret, or to all storm the walls together, are neither of them ideal. Yet with the news you bring, I think we cannot wait much longer. We must do something."

"You have a plan?"

"I have a plan, but a plan of desperation, risky for all of us."

"So tell us, then."

THEY STOOD ON THE EDGE of the clearing, facing the ogres' fortress. Krinneth considered the attack they were about to make; Lithlannon was taking a monumental risk, more of a risk for herself than for them. He had argued with her, but she had made him see that this plan, however dangerous, still represented their best chance of success.

Lithlannon and two others moved quietly and carefully out into the clearing; Krinneth would have wished to be with them, but he knew quite well that however much he had learned from the Elves, he still could not remain unseen and move as quietly as they, and Lithlannon's very life depended on moving quietly and remaining unseen.

The ogre chieftain had had his people clear the ground for some distance around the fortress to prevent anyone from creeping up unseen. But they had not done any more than they were forced to do and had carelessly left a few roots and stumps here and there. These, along with the natural humps and hollows of the ground, permitted enough cover for an Elf to move in.

Ogres, unlike goblins, do not take well to regimentation. When an ogre gives a command to another ogre, the ogre under command usually tries to think of a means to carry out the command with the least amount of work. Ogres standing sentry, therefore, can almost be depended upon to handle their duties in a slovenly and half-hearted fashion.

As a result, Lithlannon and her group could slip right up to the walls without being noticed. Krinneth himself had tried to watch them all the way, but lost sight of them in the dimness about halfway. Soon, they were standing at the wall. Lithlannon pressed her hands against the wall, while the two with her nocked arrows and looked up at the wall.

The distance was sufficient that Krinneth saw the ogre on the wall moving and pointing, saw one of the Elves loose an arrow, before he heard the ogre's shout.

He looked at Holvannon, then shouted the order. He and the other Elves were at once running across the clearing toward the wall. As he ran, Krinneth wondered about the look in Holvannon's eye; the Elf had never liked him, and liked him less now that he was put under

Krinneth's orders. Well, that was a thing which would have to be dealt with another time; now they faced a battle.

Suddenly, with a rending crash, a section of the wall split, broke asunder, and flew inwards. There were immediate cries of alarm from the ogres and the Elves, taking advantage of the momentary hesitation, rushed in.

They had chosen a place almost directly in front of the leader's headquarters. His guards were awake and watching, but they were torn between orders to hold to their posts and curiosity about what kind of force it was that could smash the logs of the walls like kindling.

The bravery of ogres is greatly connected to their dimness of wit, almost an inability to perceive danger. What might have thrown goblins into a panic, therefore, merely made ogres stop and stare. But at this hour, there were few ogres about, save for those on the walls and those watching the chieftain's quarters. There was no stirring from the barracks as yet.

As he rushed through the gap in the walls at the head of the Elves, Krinneth saw Lithlannon sagging in the arms of one of the two Elves who had been her escort at the wall. No wound that he could see, fortunately, but the power she had used in her spell would have weakened her severely. For an instant he wanted to take her in his arms, carry her off to somewhere safe, but he knew she depended upon him to see to the carrying out of the task once she had done her part. Her escort would see her to safety.

They swept up to the ogre chieftain's quarters, where the guards had recovered their wits and were readying their weapons.

Krinneth had Grothrion out and ready, but several Elves behind him had bows bent and ready, and he heard and saw the arrows zip past him. One ogre, sorely wounded, staggered around in a small circle and fell. Another, raising a short, thick-bladed sword, leaped forward, but fell and landed on his face, unmoving. Then Krinneth and the first of the Elves were among them, and there was little room left for arrows.

An ogre swung a huge spiked club at him. He dodged away, knowing that he might well catch the blow on his shield, but that he would probably suffer a broken arm for it, and be driven so far off-balance that he would be an easy target for the next blow. As the club swept by, he jumped in himself, striking with Grothrion. The ogre staggered, but the club came back in a backhand stroke. Krinneth ducked under that and struck again. Suddenly, that ogre was gone, and another stood in front of him. He struck, then dodged back from a thrust of a huge spear. In the same moment, an Elf leaped in and thrust a sword into the ogre's side. The monster roared and fell.

No enemy remained in front of them, and Krinneth bounded for the door. That had been the agreed plan, that he and five others should attempt to get inside as quickly as possible. Another five were to go in as soon as the guards were all taken care of, while the rest remained outside to deal with the other ogres.

The ogre-smell was extremely strong inside the building, and vied with several other stenches of various sorts. There was no immediate sign of the ogre-chief, then in the blink of an eye, he was there before them, having come out of a room off the main corridor.

Ogres are slow of wit, but an ogre-chief is usually somewhat quicker than most, and he wasted no time speaking. He carried a spear with a blade as wide as a shovel, and he thrust at Krinneth in a quick motion. Krinneth caught the thrust on his shield, warding it off, and struck in return with the flail. The ogre leaped backward with a quickness, surprising in one of his bulk, then thrust again.

Now one of the other Elves was up beside Krinneth; this being an ogre-dwelling, there was room for two, even though one of them was wielding a flail.

Again Krinneth avoided the thrust, but the ogre had his spear back quickly enough that Krinneth had no opening for a return blow. The Elf beside him thrust with his own spear, but the ogre parried that in a quick twisting motion that almost tore the spear from the Elf's hands.

In a motion which followed from his parry, the ogre thrust his spear forward, and though the Elf tried to dodge away, the ogre's spear pulled back with blood on the blade.

Krinneth, in the meantime, was not idle. As the ogre was parrying the spear-thrust, he swung Grothrion in a backhand motion, so that as the ogre's side was unprotected in the instant of his own thrust, the flail struck home in his side.

The ogre staggered back, and Krinneth stepped in, swinging again. His first blow had been true, and before the ogre could recover from that, the second blow had landed. The ogre reeled back against the wall and went down.

The Elf who had been fighting beside Krinneth was also down, but another Elf was kneeling beside him. Krinneth stepped over to the ogre. This was the leader, but where was the Shield? Perhaps he had merely heard the sounds of battle, taken the first weapon to hand, and come forth. In that case, the Shield ought to be in his room.

Krinneth went to the room from which the ogre had emerged.

If he had thought the ogre-smell was strong in the corridor, here it was near overwhelming. The room was in near darkness, and there was what looked like a nest of hides along one wall, probably the ogre's bed. There were other things in the room as well, chests and boxes, but he had no time for a treasure-hunt. Things were strewn on the floor just where the ogre dropped them, and the Shield was not immediately apparent.

Two more Elves were behind him now.

"Do you see the Shield anywhere?" Krinneth asked as he surveyed the room.

Both answered in the negative. "Well, let us wade through this mess."

The mess on the floor consisted of various things, useful items, worn clothing, dishes, old shoes. One elf suddenly called in a low voice, and Krinneth turned. The Elf had lifted up an old tunic, and under it shone the onyx settings of the Shield.

"Ah, good. Let us be gone, then!"

When they got out the door, they found the Elves were fighting desperately against a growing number of ogres. Above the roar of the battle, Krinneth shouted, "Find Holvannon! Let us withdraw, quickly!"

The ogres had been trying to work their way around the Elves to surround them, but as yet, they had not quite managed it. Under a leader, they would probably not have allowed a single Elf to escape, but as it was, it was a near thing. The Elves moved back to the breach in the wall, fighting all the way. Once they had moved into that gap, they continually shortened their front, while some of those behind took up bows to shoot arrows into the ogres battering at the line.

Still, it was some time before the last of them could disengage and begin to run across the clearing again. Krinneth had wielded Grothrion to great effect, and was one of those in the final line when they at last turned and ran.

The ogres were a little slow to understand what was happening, so that the Elves were a few steps ahead of them when they began to pursue.

Chapter Twenty-Five
THE CENTAURS

They came at last to the place where they had agreed to gather. It was far enough away from the fortress that the Elves could leave the ogres far behind, and yet near enough that all save perhaps the most grievously wounded could reach it.

The gnomes had kept a small fire going, and had cooked food, as well as preparing bandages for the wounded and the like. Krinneth was pleased to see that several other Elves were already there; they had scattered in their flight, intending to add to the confusion of the ogres. He was not too concerned that Lithlannon had not yet arrived because he knew the Elves who were with her would have to almost carry her.

He took a small cup of hot broth from Varti, then sat down to wait and watch. He himself had taken only a few scratches, so he had no great need of bandaging, but the broth was excellent, and it was only when he began to drink it that he realized how hungry he had been.

While he had been taking his broth, three more Elves had arrived, and as though that were a signal, more of them came slipping into the firelight. Krinneth watched, worrying, until finally a pair of Elves brought Lithlannon in. One was carrying her over his shoulders, and she seemed dreadfully limp. Krinneth sprang to his feet and rushed over.

The Elf laid her down carefully, then smiled at Krinneth. "No, she is not hurt, only wearied from the exertion of her spell. And she would insist on trying to run along with us for the first little distance."

Krinneth smiled back at him, then sat down beside Lithlannon, taking one of her hands in his. He had sat that way for a little while when he heard a voice behind him. "By the Great Tree outlander, I think she does not need you pawing at her!"

He stood, turning, and his hand went immediately to the handle of Grothrion protruding from his belt. Holvannon was sneering at him. Krinneth looked him up and down, then shrugged and turned away.

"Ha! Even with the weapon of power stolen from the dead, you fear me!"

Krinneth turned slowly back. "Holvannon, with all the fighting we have done this night, I expect we are all tired and on edge. Let us say rather that I forgive you."

Had he been thinking clearly at the time, Krinneth would have realized that this was a bad choice of words.

"Forgive me?" Holvannon's nostrils flared and his eyes blazed. "You would forgive me? Outlander, you are a fool, as well as everything else! It is you who ought to beg my forgiveness!" His sword flickered free of the scabbard. "Down on your knees, outland scum! Beg, and see if you can convince me to forgive you!"

By this time, some of the others had noticed what was happening; several of them stepped between Krinneth and Holvannon, while some took Holvannon by the arms to prevent him doing injury to anyone. They began to murmur to him, trying to calm him down, while a few others led Krinneth away as well.

During all this, Holvannon shouted, "When the war is over, outlander, and when the goblins are defeated, then I shall deal with you!"

Then his friends had taken him out of sight of Krinneth, and he became quieter. Nothing further came of it, though Holvannon carefully avoided Krinneth from that time on. For his own part, Krinneth did not try to force his company on the Elf.

By the middle of the next day, twenty-two Elves had come into the camp. They assumed that most of the others were dead. Lithlannon was rather pale, partly because of the exertion, partly because of the knowledge that so many had died in the carrying out of the plan. At last, when it was no longer likely that any of the remaining Elves would be arriving, she spoke to them.

"So, we have achieved what we set out to do, though the cost was terribly high. Now all that is left for us to do is to return to Arlith-ysterven, and hope that our deeds will have some effect on the war."

In fact, they did not leave until the next day. In the morning Lithlannon called Krinneth to her and handed him the Shield. "Krinneth, I think it would be best if you bear this."

"A foretelling, lady?"

She smiled. "Of a sort, Krinneth. But as with all our knowledge of the Shield, it is too vague for any proper description. It is only a feeling I have that the Shield ought to be borne by you, the one who wields the flail Grothrion."

He bowed. "Then I will carry it gladly, lady."

They marched toward the lowlands. Because some of them were wounded, they could not at first march so quickly as they were used to, yet they were not unsatisfied with the speed of their march.

On the third day, they came across another centaur. Unlike Khorin, this one was a female, but like Khorin, she was being attacked by a band of goblins and was defending herself with a short dagger.

Once again, with hardly a word spoken, the Elves attacked the goblins. There were twenty of them, but intent on their prey, they were unaware of the Elves until the attack was well begun. Several of them went down almost immediately, and the others panicked and fled. After the Elves had made sure of the dead, they looked round to find the centaur gone.

Lithlannon looked at Krinneth and grinned. "And there is gratitude, I suppose."

"Or perhaps, not having seen many Elves before, she had no idea that falling into our hands would be better than falling into the hands of the goblins."

They continued their march. The next day as they were travelling, the scouts who were watching their back-trail sent word that the centaurs were coming. And indeed they were. Shortly after the arrival of the warning from the scouts, they heard many hooves and suddenly centaurs were all around them, trampling and stamping.

Khorin himself approached the leaders of the Elven band.

"Hit seems Hi hwonce more must thankh you ffor assistance," he said.

Lithlannon shrugged. "It was nothing at all. We saw a creature being attacked by goblins, and we came to her aid. We would have done as much for anyone."

"Hennh, hexactly so. Hand yet, hwe hweary hof this business hof khoblins hin the hills harrassing hus. Hwe have gathered han harmy to go down hand deal hwith them. Hand hif Hi ham not mistaken, you go in the same direction. Hiff you hwill, hwe will haccompany you."

Lithlannon looked around at the centaurs, males, females, and colts. All the older ones were armed, many with short bows, some with swords, spears, and axes, and a few only with clubs. "How many are you?"

Khorin smiled. "Honly habout ffiffty now, but messages have been sent to hother herds. By the time hwe leave the hills, hwe hwill be ha thousand hor more. Yes, Helff-lady, hwe hare serious habout hall this."

Lithlannon smiled in return. "We will welcome you, then."

That same evening, Michmesh disappeared. They thought he had merely gone off visiting the small people in the neighbourhood, but he did not reappear in the morning. They went on without him.

In the next three days, numbers of centaurs joined them, so that by that time the Elves were marching at the head of a small but growing army.

On the evening of that third day, though, a bird came in with a message for the Elves. Lithlannon read it, and her face grew grim. "The fortresses are all taken or besieged, and the goblins are marching on Arlith-ysterven." She looked around at them. "This message is a few days old, so that by now the city is almost certainly besieged. It is even possible that we will not arrive in time to help, but rather only in time to die in her ruins. What would you that we do?"

"There is no choice," declared Holvannon. "We will march and we will fight, and perhaps we will die, but if we die, we will have made the goblins pay heavily for their victory. Or is there any here who is afraid? Let him go and leave us to our work."

Lithlannon frowned at him. "Strong words, Holvannon. And yet, ought we to throw our lives away on a wasted gesture, one that even the goblins will have forgotten in a few years' time?"

"What else would you suggest? Shall we live when our King is slain by goblin swords, and our great city destroyed? And if you say we should live in spite of that, then why should we live? So that the last twenty Elves in all Faerie may live the lives of hunted beasts in the wood until the last of us are finally tracked down and slain by goblins or others?"

Lithlannon raised a hand. "Holvannon, I have not yet given up hope of arriving at Arlith-ysterven in time for the battle. It only occurs to me that it might be as well to avoid the city, to seek out all the Elves who dwell in the villages and farms, and perhaps gather them together so that we might build our people anew in some far part of Faerie. What I would say is that if there are any here who doubt the wisdom of going to fight a nearly lost battle at Arlith-ysterven, they may go with our blessing, and none will call them coward in my hearing." As she spoke those last words, she looked directly at Holvannon.

Unwilling to meet her challenge, he dropped his eyes. Krinneth, who was somewhat curious as to how the other Elves felt about

Lithlannon's offer, would have liked to look around to see, but felt it would be less than polite.

She waited a bit, then smiled. "So be it, then. We all go."

At that moment, Khorin approached her. "Lady, you speak hwell. You know, there his ha hway ffor you hand your people to travel ffaster."

"And what would that be?"

"Hwe centaurs hare many, hand hwe hare hused to travelling ffast. Hwe have been going more slowly with you so has not to houtrun you. But hif heach hof you hwere to mount hwone hof hus, hwe could go much more swifftly."

Her eyes widened slightly. "Indeed?"

"Hindeed, Lady."

"Would the burden not slow you?"

"Ha little, perhaps. But hif you ride the strongest hwones hof hus, and change mounts ffrom time to time, Hit should be less diffficult."

She grinned. "We will do it, then, Khorin. And my thanks to you."

He shrugged, the rippling shrug which began with his shoulders and caused his whole body to move. "Hwe go to have hour revenge hon the khoblins, and you go to ffight the khoblins as hwell. Hwhy should hwe not help you?"

Later, when most of the rest had sought their beds for the night, Lithlannon spoke to Krinneth. "Why do you come? This is not your fight."

"But it is, lady. Did I not promise you nine years of service? And the nine years are not yet over. If you go to this fight, then I must as well."

"Only because of that you come to what is likely to be a doomed fight? If I free you from your oath, Krinneth, what would you do?"

"My lady, I would still follow you. Oath or no, having spent so long with your people, I could hardly turn my back on you now."

She was quiet for a long while, then she spoke again. "Why do you call me 'my lady?' I had thought we were too close comrades for such formality."

"When you talk to me of my oath and service, I speak as soldier to commander. A long-established habit, I suppose; one can be on friendly terms with one's commanders, share food and drink with them, but when time comes to speak of orders and plans, one treats them with the deference due their rank."

She nodded, and a smile started on her lips, but died quickly. For a long time she stood in silence, with her face showing nothing, only a hint of trouble in her eyes.

"Lithlannon, what is it? What troubles you?"

Her eyes suddenly focussed on him with a start. "Oh! What troubles me? Ah, Krinneth, it is a feeling which leads me on twisted paths of thought. I could almost wish that you were not so concerned for your obligations in the world outside, that I might tempt you to stay with me. And yet, if you were the sort of man who might be tempted away from his obligations, no matter how inconvenient they might be, would you still be the sort of man I would wish to keep with me? If you can understand all that." She ended up with a small laugh.

"I understand it all too well, Lithlannon."

"Tell me, Krinneth, if you ride out of here and find that your obligations have been forgotten, that none remember your promises of service, would you come back?"

Krinneth was somewhat surprised; he had never before heard Lithlannon speak so, and he knew that his leaving would be as difficult for her as it would be for him.

"Lithlannon, Lithlannon, what should I say? There is time and to spare before we will know anything about that, and there is much that must come first. Indeed, we may not survive the coming battle with the goblins, and anything I might say would be wasted breath.

"But you cannot have missed noticing my feelings toward you; if I am free, I will come back."

The next day, the wild ride began. The centaurs wore no saddles, stirrups, or bridles, so they left their riders to cling tightly with their legs and try to maintain their balance. Overhanging branches were the greatest difficulty, but they soon learned to watch the heads of their mounts, and when the centaur ducked, they would as well.

They travelled quickly, as Khorin had promised, pausing from time to time for the Elves to switch from one centaur's back to another. Then they were off again. They also paused once or twice during the day for a general rest, and when it became too dark to risk the tree-branches, they would camp until first light.

The next day, Michmesh suddenly returned. He slipped quietly into camp as was his habit, but rather than going to the fire to get something to eat, he came directly to Lithlannon. "Lady," he said, "I am bringing you some reinforcements."

"Reinforcements?"

"Yes, Lady. You will be remembering how I have been telling you of the goblins and their doings in the hills? There are many who are having grudges against the goblins, and will be coming with us to be having revenge."

"How many, and where are they?"

Michmesh gave his little shrug. "A thousand or more, and they are all around us. But most of them are not as myself, and are a little shy of coming out in the sight of so many. You will see us when you come to the battle, though."

"I thank you, Michmesh, and the King will wish to thank you as well."

Again the shrug. "Elf-people have been being friendly to us always, goblins have always been being trouble. If the Elves will be being defeated, will not the Little Folk also be suffering?

"I have also been spreading the word, Lady, and there will be being others who may be joining us as well."

For all that, though, the only result that was seen was that the next day a band of centaurs joined them, centaurs bearing a group of about three hundred Facherlein. The Little Makers were all armed with sword, shield, bow, and spear, and all expressed their desire to have revenge on the goblins.

Finally, when they were near to the city, Khorin's scouts brought back word of the situation. "Hit hwould seem," he said, "that the situation his grave. There hare ffires hin several quarters hof the city, hand the khoblins hare making continual hassaults. Heven hiff hwe travel has ffast has hwe have been doing, there may not be much to save ffrom the city hat the hend."

"What then? Would you go back to the hills? Khorin, I thank you for your help thus far. Whatever you might decide; it is not your city, but we ourselves will carry on."

"Hennh, you halmost hinsult me, Helff lady!" But the laughter in his eyes showed Khorin was far from being insulted. "Hi but tell you hwhat the situation his! Hwe Centaurs did not come down ffrom the hills to merely look on numerous khoblins and slink back hagain. Hit his ffor you to decide hwether you hwish to haccompany hus hin hour hattack!"

"Or do you accompany us? Well, then, let us plan to make the best of what forces we have."

Chapter Twenty-Six
THE BATTLE FOR ARLITH-YSTERVEN

The centaurs, some of them still carrying the mounted Elves, galloped down toward the city, fully into the surprised goblins. Elves had slipped through the woods and slain the guards and sentries who were to have given warning of any approaching foe. But the goblins, knowing all the Elves were shut up in the city, had expected no relieving forces.

As a result, the sudden appearance of the centaurs, armed and ready for battle, took them completely by surprise.

It was even worse when they found Grothrion among them, striking right and left, felling a goblin with every stroke. They had heard of the recovery of Grothrion, of its appearance in the hand of a hero, and fearsome tales of its might had passed among them. Its actual appearance among them was, therefore, even more terrible.

In the first few moments, it seemed possible they might be easily driven away. But the hosts which Shtavrak had led into this war were many, and though some fled immediately, there were sufficient numbers of goblins that the Elves and centaurs were still easily outnumbered.

But aside from the Elves, the centaurs, and the gnomes, came a host of others. Hundreds of Puchlein armed with their small bows and arrows flew here and there and wreaking havoc on the goblins; there were others, folk of the same size as the Puchlein, but without wings, who also wielded bows and arrows, and some even small swords. There were stout little folk, like dwarves, but smaller, but when many of them attacked a single goblin, they could still do serious damage. And there were many others as well, all of them small, all of them still able for all that to strike a blow against the goblins. Even so, they were still not sufficient to drive off the goblins, and it soon became apparent.

The Elves inside the city, however, when they saw the goblins attacked from outside, sallied forth hastily to join the battle. Even then, the battle was for a long time, barely even. Neither side could immediately gain the upper hand, though here and there one side or the other prevailed.

Shortly after the initial charge, Krinneth had dismounted. He was quite proficient at fighting while mounted. Even fighting without being able to guide his mount was not too serious a handicap. But with fighting while riding a mount who was also fighting, and thus to be merely carried here and there at the whims of that mount, he decided he would do better on his own two feet.

He thus joined himself to a pair of Elves who had made the same decision, and they went to fight among the centaurs. As they fought, other Elves joined them from time to time. Including, eventually, Lithlannon herself.

There came a brief lull in the fighting, and Lithlannon grasped him by the arm. "A moment, Krinneth! Let us see if we can use our strength more wisely."

She looked around, pulling several other Elves out of the fight as well. Then she pointed with her sword. "There!" she cried. "Let us make our way there!"

Looking where she was pointing, Krinneth saw the standard of the King of the Goblins bobbing over the fray.

He nodded. Instead of going immediately, Lithlannon got the attention of several centaurs. Then the mixed band moved.

Even so, it might have gone hard with them, for the goblins around that banner were the largest and the strongest, members of the King's bodyguard, as well as bodyguards of other chiefs. They could be depended on to fight on, even against bad odds, for the protection of their masters. In front of these was a thick mass of other goblins who, while perhaps not so hardy as the bodyguards, were still ready and willing to fight. The presence of the King and the bodyguards behind them was a stronger inducement to fight and fight well.

However, as they were charging at the goblins, the Elves and centaurs heard a strange collection of noises, hissing, thumping, and flapping. A dark shadow passed over their heads, and Krinneth looked up. He barely caught a glimpse of a wide pair of beating wings and a short stout body, leaking clouds of steam and smoke, driving inexorably on.

He smiled slightly to himself, despite the fact they were about to throw themselves into a heavy battle, for he recognized the gnomes' flying machine. A moment later, the machine crashed into the ranks of the goblins. This was something strange, something unexpected, something unexplained, coming at the moment when the goblins were facing a fierce battle with the Elves. It shook them, and their captains had no time to reassure them, with their clubs and whips and threats of dire punishment, before the Elves and centaurs were upon them.

Then the goblins found themselves facing not merely Elves and centaurs, but the flail Grothrion, of whom dreadful tales were told. It had wrought great devastation among their people in the time when the flail's wielder had fallen in Derdrona, and the tales which were told of Grothrion now said it was even more fearsome. One rumour among the goblins had it that Grothrion had slept for a hundred years, and had woken hungering for goblins, so that now it was more to be feared than ever before.

And what of that flying monster which had crashed into their ranks? Where had that fell beast come from? Did it portend some magic against which their shamans were helpless? And if that were so, what else might they face? Krinneth and his companions knew nothing of this at the time. They could tell no difference in the determination of these goblins, who still snarled defiance at them, still stood and fought, still leaped at them with bloody weapons, still struck with skill where an opening presented itself.

But whatever power there might be in the flail, no goblin could stand against it. Grothrion struck unerringly, and when the flail struck, a goblin fell. Goblins fell back and edged away from him, as he continued to advance. Yet some goblins held, on each side of him, and though at first Elves and centaurs came in to fill the gap behind him, at last their force itself was stretched too thin, and Krinneth was suddenly aware he was standing alone within a ring of goblins, none of whom cared to approach too near him.

Once or twice, bold ones tried to come at Krinneth from behind, but he always turned just before they could make their final attack. It took a little longer for them to think of using bows or javelins, and even then it was the vituperative insistences of their captains and sergeants which led them to take action.

The first few arrows glanced off his mail, or were warded off by the shield, then one struck home in his left arm, shot from behind. He was just about to fling himself at the ring of goblins, reasoning they would be less likely to shoot when they might well hit one of their own, when suddenly their ranks parted to let a large goblin through, and the shooting ceased. At first Krinneth did not recognize who stood there, then the goblin pushed back his helmet. Shathka grinned at him.

"I promised, did I not, that you and I would meet again?" He pushed his helmet back down on his head, raised his sword, and charged.

Krinneth caught the first blow on the Shield, but the goblin danced back away from his return blow. They circled each other then for a little, seeking an opening. Shathka feinted twice, but saw Krinneth was too prepared each time. For his part, Krinneth watched and waited for an opening, feeling the blood running from his wound, feeling himself weakening. In a while it would be too late, and he would fall due to loss of blood, and Shathka would triumph.

He staggered, emphasizing the stagger a little, so that he almost went down on one knee; Shathka leaped in with an inarticulate cry, sword sweeping down. In the last moment, Krinneth brought the Shield up, warding off the blow, then swung Grothrion around in a sideward stroke. The flail caught the goblin in the side, sending him staggering back and almost down, but from somewhere Shathka drew the energy to bring himself back into the battle.

He was angry, though, and he attacked with more strength than skill, striking heavy blows against the Shield as though to smash his way through. For the first moments, Krinneth was busy warding off the sword-strokes of the goblin-chief, then at last he could reply with a stroke of his own.

The flail caught Shathka in the side again, and he almost fell. His attack ceased, and Krinneth swung an overhand stroke at him, which rang off his shield. Then, in desperation, feeling himself weakening seriously, he swung a backhand blow. Shathka, still shaken from the first two blows, still tried to interpose his shield.

He was not quite successful; he staggered two paces sideward, still keeping his feet, then he fell and did not move. Krinneth, realizing this would shortly mean renewed attack with arrows and javelins, flung himself forward toward the ring of goblins.

As he did so, Krinneth saw a centaur whizzing past him, raising a large spear, and on the other side was Holvannon, sword ready. The others had broken through. He remembered little more of the battle, mere disordered scraps of fighting, with no knowledge of how he had come from one place to another. The next thing Krinneth knew, the sun was setting, the goblins were fleeing, and a centaur at his side was trying to tell him, in a very thick accent, that he ought to have his shoulder seen to. He remembered the world spinning, remembered going down on one knee, then he fell.

Krinneth awoke and knew something was strange. He tried hard for a few moments to think what it was, but though he knew it ought to be obvious, it did not seem so. He felt a little tired, which possibly accounted for it. And his wound—-!

He was immediately aware of the fact his wound was little more than a nagging discomfort, not the pain it ought to have been. He remembered Lithlannon having said, once before, that because of the healing she had done on him at the Westermoor, his wounds would always tend to heal quickly. Did that power still remain with him?

He sat up, and a muscle in his back caught a bit, causing him to gasp with pain. Then he was seated on the edge of his pallet, breathing deeply. He looked around; it seemed the great hall to the King in Arlith-ysterven had been turned into a hospital for the wounded, and there were several others there as well. Some looked to be in serious condition, others less so, and there were Elves, walking up and down the rows of pallets, offering a little drink here, changing a bandage there.

One woman saw him sitting up and hurried over. "You are recovered, then?"

"There is a little pain in my shoulder," Krinneth winced as he carefully felt his shoulder, "but I think I ought to be able to move. Ought I to be recovered already?"

She shrugged. "All I know is that the Lady Lithlannon told us that you probably needed no treatment, that the healing she had done on you long ago would likely be sufficient. And then I saw you sitting up, as you ought not to be doing with a wound such as that, so I thought you were recovered."

Krinneth shook his head. "Recovering, but not yet completely recovered. Where might I find something to eat?"

She frowned at him. "We should never hear the last of it if we sent you off half-healed to find something to eat. Stay here, and I will bring you something."

"No need. I can get up." He pushed himself up, slowly. She put a hand on his chest and pushed him back. To his surprise, he found he could not rise, and indeed, she continued to push until he was lying on his back again.

"You see?" She smiled at him as she spoke. "You are not so strong yet as you think. Now lie there, and I will be back soon." She hurried away.

Krinneth did not feel tired, but his eyes fluttered open to see the Elf-woman looking down on him, smiling, with a bowl in one hand and a piece of bread in the other.

"Did I sleep?" he asked.

She laughed. "If I had left the last bowl of broth for you to eat, it would have been stone cold by now. Here, can you hold these by yourself?"

Krinneth sat up again; this time the pain was much less. He took the bread and the bowl of broth and began to eat. He had thought he could eat more, but by the time he finished the broth, he was no longer hungry. The Elf-woman came by again and picked up the bowl and spoon. He caught her gently by the arm as she drew away from him. "Would you be able to take a message for me?"

"I can at the least pass it on to another."

"Then tell Lithlannon that I am mending."

Her smile faded. "The Lady Lithlannon fought in the battle, as you know. After the battle, she went about using her power to heal whoever she could heal, and now she herself is sleeping. I would not wake her, not if the King himself demanded it."

Krinneth smiled. "Then neither will I demand it. But leave a message for her when she awakes, if you would."

The Elf-woman bobbed her head swiftly. "That I can do, and I will."

"Thank you."

KRINNETH AND LITHLANNON were gathered again in the King's Quarters. "We are free of danger from the goblins for some time now. Shtavrak's body was found on the battlefield, and for a little while, at least they will be involved in choosing a new king. But the cost has been heavy."

Lithlannon nodded. "Yes. We have lost many. Holvannon is dead; Vohalton, for all our healing powers, yet lingers between life and death; and there are many others as well."

Krinneth was quiet. Holvannon had never been a friend. In fact, he had promised a final meeting with weapons when the war with the goblins was done. For all that, though, he had been a doughty fighter, and if war came again, he would be missed.

Something occurred to him. "We found the Shield, and I bore it into this battle, yet it seemed no more than a shield. Perhaps I am not the one who ought to bear it."

The King smiled. "Regarding that, who can say? We still know little of the Shield, even as little as we ever knew. But think of this; your search for the Shield led you to the folk who allied themselves to us in our need, and without them we would surely not have prevailed. And also, whatever power it may or may not have, the Shield provided a rallying point for the Elves, and when it was seen on your arm as you charged to battle, it did much to hearten our warriors to the last effort. And perhaps that was all that the old lore meant, that the Elves needed a symbol of their hope, and that the search for that symbol might well lead to the finding of allies."

Krinneth sighed. "I know little enough of wisdom and lore, and if what you say is true, I would rather fight with weapons of the hand. At least there I am somewhat more sure of where I stand."

KRINNETH WAS SEATED in his own quarters, puzzling out the meaning of an old scroll on history of the Elves, when the Facherlein came knocking on his door. "Come in!" he called, and watched the three come in, a little diffidently.

Varti spoke. "Lord, we come to tell you that it is time for us to be leaving."

"Ah." Krinneth could think of nothing to say to that, since he had no idea why the Little folk had stayed so long.

"Yes. We have stayed with you for some time. We have even helped you, I think. But now it is time for us to be going, to be returning to our own folk."

"We will miss you, Varti."

The Facherlein's eyes glowed. "Will you indeed? True or not, it is kind of you to say so. And you have been very patient with us, with our inventions which worked, and the many which did not."

"Ah," said Krinneth, recalling the steaming flapping machine which had hit the goblin ranks ahead of them, making their charge that much more effective. "Some were very helpful indeed."

"Good, good. And Lord, if you should ever need our skills again, you have only to send for us and we will come."

"Thank you."

The three shouldered their packs, bowed low, and went out.

Chapter Twenty-Seven

THE HOMECOMING OF KRINNETH SON OF DARUN

Krinneth rode again the winding trail around the mere towards Dhahal's land. Somehow, he was not particularly happy to be coming home at last.

Lithlannon had come to him and said a brief goodbye before he left Arlith-ysterven. The King had also come out to bid him farewell, and Vohalton told him with a grin that he would be welcome at dinner any time. When he had ridden a little distance, he had turned to wave; the King and Vohalton were still standing there, but Lithlannon had been nowhere to be seen.

Krinneth had felt a little anger then; could she not stay to see him off? But the anger was quickly replaced by a realization that, little as he wished to leave Faerie, she wished even less to see him go.

So now, here he was, riding nearer and nearer to his home, and feeling less and less happy about it. He reached down and touched the handle of Grothrion at his belt; Quarannon had bid him take the flail, for it had been given to Krinneth, and it had been well-earned. The Shield was slung at his saddle horn as well; no scryings of the Elves had told of any evil happenings to occur if the Shield was sent away, and it had been agreed that Krinneth had earned the Shield as well.

There was a sudden movement in the brush ahead, and two ponies dashed out, each bearing a young boy, and both rode furiously along the way toward Dhahal's castle.

Curious, he rode over the to brush where they had been concealed. There were the remains of a small campfire, but obviously one which had been burning for a long while. There was evidence they and their horses had been there for some time, probably weeks, and there was a small shelter made of brush to protect them from the worst of the weather.

"So they have been here for a long while, and immediately upon my approach, they ride away. Were they watching for me? But if that were so, why did they not stay to welcome me? Do they go to the castle to see that a welcome is prepared? Perhaps. And yet..."

Something about it felt wrong. He resolved to be wary and rode on. As he rode, he argued with himself. "Be wary? Of Dhahal? Now why would I feel thus? And yet, think how the people treated me when I came back visiting, as though I had been changed into something different, as though at any moment I might transform myself into a monster, or as though I were myself a warlock willing to cast dread spells on them. And yet it was Dhahal himself who worked to change their minds; has he been so changed in the past three years?"

PEOPLE WERE WORKING in the fields. As before, when they saw him, they crossed their fingers to ward off evil. As before, Krinneth pretended not to see. He continued to ride up to the castle, wondering, as he had wondered many times in the last few days, what would his reception be? How long would it take before people became used to him once more, and ceased to treat him as some strange being beyond their ken?

He saw there were two people standing in the gateway, and when he drew closer, he recognized them for Gwathlinn and her fiance. He amended that; they must be wed long since. He considered that since they were waiting for him, the two youngsters must have been ordered to warn them of his approach. But if Gwathlinn and her husband were there, where was Dhahal?

He came closer; a dozen pikemen lined the path, six to a side, to honor him as he rode in.

He came at last to where Gwathlinn and Langeth stood waiting and watching. There was a watchful wariness in their faces, as though they were concerned about him. Perhaps it was merely the concern of those greeting a man newly returned from Faerie.

He halted his mount and waited. Surprisingly, it was Gwathlinn who spoke first. "Krinneth, you swore oaths of service to my father. Will you also swear them to my husband?"

He knew now that something was dreadfully amiss here. "Dhahal is dead?"

"Yes." A bare response, with no elucidation.

"What of Dhahal's heirs?"

This time Langeth spoke up. "We are Dhahal's heirs."

"His sons?"

Langeth shrugged. "Dhahal died while hunting; a wild arrow shot in haste. None of his sons being immediately available. I therefore took it upon myself to exercise leadership, lest any enemies profit by our disarray."

"And after?"

"What then? I had already set myself up as leader, and I felt I was owed something for keeping Dhahal's lands intact. I am therefore the lord of the steading. And the question still remains, Krinneth, will you swear your oath to me?"

Krinneth felt a surge of anger. He had his doubts about this 'accident' which had befallen Dhahal, and to top it off, this fellow was demanding he swear the same oaths as he had sworn to Dhahal.

"And if I do not?"

Langeth made a signal, and the pikemen beside the road slanted their pikes toward Krinneth. "I had hoped you might be reasonable, Krinneth. My only alternative is to have you slain."

Krinneth looked at the pikemen surrounding him. Like all the people of Dhahal's estates, they were wary of this man who had come back from Faerie. He read the fear in their faces, and that told him what to do. He sneered at them. "So, then? Have I spent the past nine years in Faerie and learned nothing? A curse on the first man to touch me in anger, a curse on him and his children and the children of his children! Ill luck will follow them forever, and sickness haunt them, until they find in death only a mercy!"

The pikemen backed away, still pointing their weapons, but with little intention of using them. Langeth snarled, "At him, men! He is only one!"

They refused to move. Langeth cursed and drew his sword.

"Hold back, Langeth! Whatever you fear from me, you are mistaken! I swore oaths to Dhahal, and with his death, I am free of them. If there is vengeance to be sought, let his sons seek it. There is nothing here for me."

But Langeth would not hear; Krinneth twitched the Shield up from where it hung at his saddle, caught it with his left hand, and warded off the first blow of Langeth's sword. By the time he had caught the second blow, he had Grothrion free from his belt and swung it in return. He struck hastily, knowing that Langeth's attack might cure the pikemen's fear, and knowing he could not escape if they turned on him.

His first blow caught Langeth high on the chest. Langeth had been wearing no armour, perhaps in an attempt at not alerting Krinneth to possible danger. Langeth dropped where he stood. Krinneth was quite sure the blow was not fatal, but he had neither the time nor the inclination to complete the job. Gwathlinn was shrieking already, and the pikemen seemed to be gathering their courage. He wheeled his horse, shouting in Elvish, "Stand back! Give us room!" As he had hoped, the pikemen took this for some sort of spell and held back, just long enough for him to kick the horse into motion back along the road which he had come.

Behind him, he heard Gwathlinn shrieking. He looked back; confusion strangled the gateway. Pikemen running around frantically, looking for leadership, while their lord lay on the ground. "And belike they will have horsemen out to pursue me as soon as they can saddle their mounts," Krinneth muttered. "Best I should have a good start before that happens."

It was that evening before he realized the direction in which he was riding; he was returning to Faerie. He thought that over.

"They will welcome me back, being a courteous people, but will they really want me? I served for nine years. I aided them in their wars, but there were others besides Holvannon who distrusted and disliked outsiders. Will they indeed take me back?"

But if he had no place at Dhahal's stead, it was unlikely he would have any place at any other stead. One of Dhahal's sons might take him in, but he would have to find Dhahal's sons, and Langeth's men would be searching for him all the while. Returning to Faerie, welcome or not, seemed only the better of several bad choices.

The next morning he looked back along his trail from the top of a rise and saw far away the glint of the sun on metal. He was being pursued for certain. He rode away. Krinneth wondered. Did Langeth so fear him, then? Or could it be that Gwathlinn was behind this, not trusting his declared disinterest, wanting to make sure Krinneth had no feeling that he was owed something, even because of an understanding, however tentative?

By nightfall, they were still behind him, though they had not closed the distance by much. They continued to dog his steps to the very edge of the mere.

AS HE RODE AROUND THE mere, he saw in the distance a rider approaching. He wondered at first who it could be, and as they drew closer to each other, he could tell by the way she rode it was Lithlannon. He wondered at that? Was she merely coming out to take her turn at being the Maid of the Westermoor? Was she perhaps aware of his coming, and was riding out to warn him away from Faerie?

At last he was close enough to see her face, and he saw she was smiling. He urged his horse into a run.

Don't miss out!

Visit the website below and you can sign up to receive emails whenever J P Wagner publishes a new book. There's no charge and no obligation.

https://books2read.com/r/B-A-EKQG-FLWWB

BOOKS 2 READ

Connecting independent readers to independent writers.

Also by J P Wagner

Avantir
The Guardian of the Sword

Talisman Series
Stonecaller
Talisman of the Winds

Standalone
The Search for the Unicorns
Railroad Rising: The Black Powder Rebellion
Maid of the Westermoor

Watch for more at www.revjpwagner.com.

About the Author

J. P. Wagner was both a sci-fi/fantasy writer and a journalist. While his editorials and informative articles could be found in publications such as the Western Producer and the Saskatoon Star Phoenix, Railroad Rising: The Black Powder Rebellion is his first published novel.

A self-proclaimed curmudgeon, but known to his family as a merry jokester, his words have brightened many lives. Sadly, J. P. Wagner passed away in 2015 before the publication of Railroad Rising: The Black Powder Rebellion.

While this may be the last book he finished before he died, it doesn't mean that this was his only book. In addition to his career in journalism, he wrote many novels throughout his lifetime. All of these works have been passed down to me, his daughter and now I will share them with you.

Read more at www.revjpwagner.com.

CPSIA information can be obtained
at www.ICGtesting.com
Printed in the USA
LVHW010938020822
724959LV00002B/199